also has Radiguet's untroubled artistic amorality. It deals with a girl of her age, who is finally freed from boarding schools to live in unchecked enjoyment with her youngish widowed father, an affectionate, civilized lightweight immoralist whose life events are composed of rather commonplace passing mistresses, picked up in his easy Champs-Elysees business world. The crux of the story, which takes place in the Midi during the father's and daughter's summer holiday *a trois* with an especially blowsy mistress, is the arrival there of the dead mother's best friend—an intelligent, forceful Parisienne, who not only falls in love with the father and easily ousts the mistress but plans to marry him and save him, at forty, from his shapeless, tarnishing life and worse future, and to bring up the girl *comme il faut*."

The New Yorker says: "Worth a dozen ordinary superfatted best sellers. A greatly gifted writer."

The Saturday Review says: "Sensational! yes; but skillfully and quietly done."

Sterling North says in the *N. Y. World Telegram* & *Sun*: "A superb story."

Newsweek says: "A born literary psychologist with

N. Y. Herald (Front page extraordinary.

John K. Hutch *Herald Tribune*: A writer of ing talent."

BONJOUR TRISTESSE

BONJOUR
TRISTESSE

FRANÇOISE SAGAN, pseud.
Françoise Quoirez

Translated from the French by
IRENE ASH

New York

E P DUTTON AND COMPANY

1955

LIBRARY OF CONGRESS CATALOG CARD NUMBER: 55-5341

PART ONE

Adieu tristesse
Bonjour tristesse
Tu es inscrite dans les lignes du plafond
Tu es inscrite dans les yeux que j'aime
Tu n'es pas tout à fait la misère
Car les lèvres les plus pauvres te dénoncent
Par un sourire
Bonjour tristesse
Amour des corps aimables
Puissance de l'amour
Dont l'amabilité surgit
Comme un monstre sans corps
Tête désappointée
Tristesse beau visage.

P. ELUARD.
(La vie immédiate.)

Chapter 1

A STRANGE melancholy pervades me to which I hesitate to give the grave and beautiful name of sorrow. The idea of sorrow has always appealed to me, but now I am almost ashamed of its complete egoism. I have known boredom, regret, and occasionally remorse, but never sorrow. Today it envelops me like a silken web, enervating and soft, and sets me apart from everybody else.

That summer, I was seventeen and perfectly happy. At that time "everybody else" was my father and his mistress, Elsa. I must explain this situation at once, or it might give a false impression. My father was forty, and had been a widower for fifteen years. He was young for his age, full of vitality and liveliness. When I left my convent school two years before and came to Paris to live with him, I soon realized that he was living with a woman. But I was slower in accepting the fact that his fancy changed every six months! But gradually his charm, my new easy life, and my own disposition, led me to fall in readily with his ways. He was a frivolous man, clever at business, always curious, quickly bored, and very attractive to women. It was easy for me to love him, for he was kind, generous, gay and fond of me. I cannot imagine a better or a more amusing companion. At the beginning of the summer I am concerned with now, he even asked me whether I would object to having Elsa along on our summer vacation. She was his mistress of the moment, a tall, red-headed girl, sensual and worldly, kindly, rather simple-minded, and unpretentious. One might have come across her any day in the studios and bars of the Champs-Elysées. I readily consented, for I knew his need of a woman, and I knew, too, that Elsa would not get in our way. Besides, my father and I were so delighted at the prospect of going away that I was in no mood to object to anything. He had rented a large white villa on the Mediterranean, for which we had been longing since the spring. It was remote and beautiful, standing on a headland jutting over the sea, hidden from the road by pine woods. A goat path led down to a small, sunny cove where the sea lapped against rust-colored rocks.

The first days were dazzling. We spent hours on the beach giving ourselves up to the hot sun, gradually assuming a healthy golden tan—except for Elsa, whose skin reddened and peeled, causing her intense agony. My father performed all sorts of complicated exercises to reduce a rounding stomach unsuitable for a Don Juan. From dawn onward I was in the water. It was cool and transparent, and I plunged wildly about in my efforts to wash away the shadows and dust of Paris. I lay stretched out on the sand, took up a handful and let it run through my fingers in soft, yellow streams. I told myself that it ran out like time. It was an idle thought, and it was pleasant to have idle thoughts, for it was summer.

On the sixth day I saw Cyril for the first time. He was hugging the coast in a small sailboat and capsized in front of our cove. I had a wonderful time helping him to rescue his things, during which he told me his name, that he was studying law, and was spending his vacation with his mother in a neighboring villa. He had a typically Latin face—very dark and very frank. There was something responsible and protective about him which I liked at once. Usually I avoided college students, whom I considered brutal, wrapped up in themselves, particularly in their youth, in which they found material for drama, or an excuse for their own boredom. I did not care for young people; I much preferred my father's friends, men of forty, who spoke to me courteously and tenderly—treated me with the gentleness of a father—or a lover. But Cyril was different. He was tall and almost beautiful, with the kind of good looks that immediately inspires one with confidence. Although I did not share my father's intense aversion to ugliness—which often led us to associate with stupid people—I did feel vaguely uncomfortable in the presence of anyone completely devoid of physical charm. Their resignation to the fact that they were unattractive seemed to me somehow indecent. For what are we looking for if not to please? I do not know if the desire to attract others comes from a superabundance of vitality, possessiveness, or the hidden, unspoken need to be reassured.

When Cyril left he offered to teach me to sail. I went up to dinner absorbed in my thoughts of him, and hardly spoke during the meal or noticed my father's nervousness. After dinner we stretched out in chairs on the terrace as usual. The sky was studded with stars. I gazed upward, vaguely hoping to see a sudden, exciting flash across the heavens, but it was early in July and too soon for shooting stars. On the terrace the crickets were chirping. There must have been thousands of them, drunk with heat and moonlight, pouring out their song all night long. I had been told they made the sound by rubbing their legs together, but I preferred to believe that it came from the throat, guttural, instinctive like the howls of cats in heat.

We were very comfortable. A few tiny grains of sand between my skin and my shirt kept me from dropping off to sleep. Suddenly my father coughed apologetically and sat up.

"Someone is coming to stay with us," he announced.

I shut my eyes in disappointment. We had been too happy; it just couldn't last!

"Hurry up and tell us who it is!" cried Elsa, always avid for gossip.

"Anne Larsen," said my father, and he turned toward me.

"I asked her to come if she was worn out by the collections and she . . . she's coming."

Anne was the last person I would have thought my father would ask to visit us. She had been a friend of my mother's, and had very little connection with my father. Just the same, when I left the convent school two years before and my father was at his wits' end about me, he had asked her to take me in hand. Within a week she had dressed me in the right clothes and taught me something about life. I remember thinking her the most wonderful person and being quite embarrassingly fond of her. But she soon managed to transfer my affections to a young man she knew. To her I owed my first taste of fashion and my first flirtation, and I was very grateful. At forty-two she was a most attractive woman, much sought after, with a beautiful face, proud, calm, reserved. This aloofness was the only complaint one could make against her. But she was kind as well as aloof. Everything about her denoted a strong will, an inner serenity which was awesome. Although divorced now, she seemed to have no lovers; but then we did not know the same people. Her friends were clever, intelligent and discreet. Ours, from whom my father demanded only good looks or amusement, were loud and insatiable. I think she rather despised us for our love of diversion and frivolity, as she despised all extremes. We had few points of contact except through the world of business and the memory of my mother. Her work was concerned with women's fashions and my father's with publicity, so they met occasionally at professional dinners. Added to this were my own determined efforts to keep in touch with her, because, although she awed me, I greatly admired her. So her unexpected appearance here worried me because of Elsa's presence and Anne's ideas on my upbringing.

Elsa went up to bed after making detailed inquiries about Anne's social position. I remained alone with my father and moved over to the steps, where I sat at his feet. He leaned forward and put his hands on my shoulders.

"Why are you so thin, darling? You look like a little wildcat. I'd like to have a lovely, buxom, fair-haired daughter with china-blue eyes and . . ."

"That's hardly the point," I said. "What made you invite Anne, and why did she accept?"

"Perhaps she wants to see your old father, you never know."

"You're not the type of man to interest Anne," I said. "She's too intelligent and has too much self-respect. And what about Elsa? Have you thought of her? Can you imagine what Elsa and Anne can talk about? I can't!"

"I'm afraid it hadn't occurred to me," he confessed. "But you're right, it's a dreadful thought. Cécile, my sweet, shall we go right back to Paris?"

He laughed softly and rubbed the back of my neck. I turned to look at him. His dark eyes gleamed; funny little wrinkles marked their edges; his mouth was turned up slightly. He looked like a faun. I laughed with him as I always did when he created complications for himself.

"My little partner in crime," he said. "What would I do without you?"

His voice was so serious yet so tender that I knew he would really have been unhappy without me. Late into the night we talked of love, of its complications. In my father's eyes they were all imaginary. He refused categorically all ideas of fidelity or serious commitments. He explained that they were arbitrary and sterile. From anyone else such views would have shocked me, but I knew that in his case they did not exclude tenderness and devotion—feelings which came all the more easily to him since he was determined that they should be transient. This conception of quick, tempestuous and passing love affairs I found enticing. I was not at the age when fidelity is attractive. And of course, I knew little of love: the meetings, the kisses, the weary aftermath.

Chapter 2

ANNE was not expected for another week, and I made the most of these last days of real freedom. We had rented the villa for two months, but I knew that once she was there it would be impossible for any of us to relax completely. Anne gave a shape to things and a meaning to words that my father and I preferred to ignore. She set a standard of good taste and fastidiousness which one could not help noticing in her sudden withdrawals, the look on her face, and her hurt silences. It was both stimulating and exhausting, but in the long run humiliating, because I could not help feeling that she was right.

On the day of her arrival we decided that my father and Elsa should meet her at the station in Fréjus. I firmly refused to go with them. In desperation my father cut all the gladioli in the garden to offer her as soon as she got off the train. My only advice to him was not to allow Elsa to carry the bouquet. After they had left I went down to the beach. It was three o'clock and the heat was overpowering. I was lying on the sand half asleep when I heard Cyril calling to me. I opened my eyes; the sky was white, shimmering with heat. I made no reply, because I did not want to speak to him, or to anyone. I was nailed to the sand by all the strength of summer heat—my arms were like lead, my mouth dry.

"Are you dead?" he said. "From over there you looked like something washed up by the sea."

I smiled. He sat down near me and my heart began to beat faster, more heavily, because his hand had just touched my shoulder. A dozen times during the past week my brilliant seamanship had cast us into the water, our arms entwined, and I had not felt the least twinge of excitement. But today the heat, my being half-asleep and his accidental touch had somehow broken down my defenses. I turned my head toward him. I was getting to know him better. He was steady, more strait-laced than is perhaps usual at his age. For this reason my family situation, our unusual domestic trio, shocked him. He was too kind or too timid to tell me, but I felt it in the oblique looks of disapproval he gave my father. It would have pleased him if I had let him know that I, too, was tormented by this situation. But I was not. In fact my only torment at that moment was the way my heart was thumping. He bent over me. I thought of the past few days, of my feeling of peace and confidence when I was with him, and I was tempted to resist the touch of his soft, full lips on mine.

"Cyril," I said. "We were so happy . . ."

But his kiss was gentle. I looked at the sky, then saw nothing but lights bursting under my closed eyelids.

The warmth, the dizziness, and the savor of our first kisses went on for a long moment. The sound of a motor horn pulled us apart guiltily. I left Cyril without a word and went up to the house. I was surprised that the car was back so soon; Anne's train could hardly have arrived as yet. But there was Anne on the terrace, just getting out of her own car.

"This is as silent as the house of the Sleeping Beauty," she said. "How brown you are, Cécile! I am so pleased to see you."

"I, too," I answered. "But have you just come from Paris?"

"I decided to drive down. And, by the way, I'm exhausted."

I showed her to her room and opened the window, hoping to catch a glimpse of Cyril's boat. It had disappeared. Anne sat down on the bed. I noticed little shadows around her eyes.

"What a delightful villa!" she said. "Where's the master of the house?"

"He's gone to meet you at the station, with Elsa."

I had put her suitcase on a chair, and when I turned around I received a shock. Her face had suddenly collapsed; her mouth was trembling.

"Elsa Mackenbourg? He brought Elsa Mackenbourg here?"

I could not think of anything to say. I looked at her, completely stupified. Was this the face I had always seen so calm and controlled? Her eyes were on me, still

I realised she saw not me but the images my words had given her. Finally she saw my expression and looked away.

"I ought to have given you a little more time before coming," she said. "But I was in such a hurry to get away and so tired."

"And now . . ." I went on like an automaton.

"Now *what?*" she said.

Her expression was purely an inquiry obliterating what had passed, as though nothing had happened.

"Well, now you're *here*," I said stupidly, rubbing my hands together. "You don't know how happy I am that you're here. Unpack and relax, and I'll be waiting for you downstairs. If you want a drink, the bar is very well stocked."

Talking incoherently, I left the room and went downstairs with my mind in a turmoil. What had caused that sudden collapse, that shocked voice, that look of anguish? I sat on a chaise-longue and closed my eyes. I tried to remember Anne's various expressions: sometimes cold, sometimes affectionate—her moods of irony, easy authority. I found myself both touched and irritated by the discovery that she was vulnerable. Was she in love with my father? Was it possible for her to love him?

He was not at all her type. He was weak, frivolous and sometimes unreliable. But perhaps it was only the fatigue of the trip—or moral indignation. I spent an hour in vain conjecture.

At five o'clock my father and Elsa arrived. I saw him getting out of the car. Again I wondered if Anne could possibly be in love with him. He walked quickly toward me, his head tilted a little backward. He was smiling. Of course it was quite possible for Anne to love him, for anyone to love him!

"Anne wasn't there," he called to me. "I hope she hasn't fallen out of the train?"

"She's in her room," I said. "She came in her car."

"No? Splendid! Then you can take up the bouquet to her!"

"Did you buy me flowers?" called Anne's voice "How sweet of you!"

She came down the stairs to meet him, cool, smiling, in a dress that showed no signs of travel. I reflected she had appeared only when she heard the car; if she had wanted to talk with me she could have come down earlier—even if only to ask about my exams, in which, by the way, I had failed. This last thought consoled me.

My father rushed up to Anne and kissed her hand.

"I stood a quarter of an hour on the station platform, holding this bunch of flowers, feeling utterly foolish. Thank goodness you're here! Do you know Elsa Mackenbourg?"

I averted my eyes.

"We must have met," said Anne, all amiability. "What a lovely room you have given me. It was most kind of you to ask me to come here, Raymond. I was exhausted."

My father gave a snort of pleasure. In his eyes everything was going well. He made conversation, uncorked
bottles. But I kept thinking, first of Cyril's passionate
face, and then of Anne's, both with the stamp of violence
on them. And I wondered if the rest of the vacation
would be as uncomplicated as my father had assumed.

This first dinner was very gay. My father and Anne
talked of the friends they had in common, who were
few, but very colorful. I was enjoying myself up to
the moment when Anne declared that my father's business partner was an idiot. He was a man who drank a
lot, but I liked him very much, and my father and I had
had memorable evenings in his company.

"But, Anne," I protested, "Lombard is a lot of fun.
He can be very amusing."

"But you've just admitted that he has his faults, and
as for his brand of humor—"

"He has perhaps not a very brilliant type of mind,
but—"

She interrupted indulgently.

"What you call types of mind are only mental ages."

I was delighted with her remark. Certain phrases fas-
cinate me with their subtle implications, even though
I may not altogether understand their meaning. I told
Anne that I wanted to write her comment in my note-
book. My father burst out laughing:

"At least you're not resentful!"

How could I be when Anne had not meant to hurt
me? I felt that she was impartial, that her judgments

did not have the sharp edge of spite. And so they were all the more effective.

The first evening Anne did not seem to notice that Elsa went quite openly into my father's bedroom. She had brought me a sweater she had designed, but would not permit any thanks. It just bored her to be thanked, she said, and as I was awkward in expressing gratitude, I was most relieved.

"I think Elsa is very nice," she remarked as I was about to leave her room to go to bed.

She looked straight at me without a smile, daring me to remember her earlier reaction; I realized I was to forget it.

"Oh yes, she's a charming girl . . . very warm-hearted," I stammered.

She laughed, and I went to bed, most upset. I fell asleep thinking of Cyril who was probably at that moment dancing in Cannes with the same kind of charming girl.

I realize that I have skipped over an important factor: the nearness of the sea with its incessant rhythm. Nor have I mentioned the four lime trees in the courtyard of my convent school and their perfume, or my father's smile as he and I stood at the railroad station three years ago when he came to take me home—his embarrassed smile because my hair was in braids and I wore an ugly, dark dress. And then on the train his sudden, triumphant joy because he saw I had his eyes, his mouth, and I was going to be for him the dearest, most marvelous of toys. I was completely inexperienced; he would show me Paris, luxury, the gay life. I dare say I owed most of my pleasures of that period to money; the pleasure of driving fast in a high-powered car, of buying a new dress, records, books, flowers. Even now I am not ashamed of indulging in these pleasures. In fact I just take them for granted. I would rather deny myself my moods of mysticism or despair than give up my indulgences. My love of pleasure seems to be the only consistent side of my character. Is it because I have not read enough? In school one reads only edifying works. In Paris there was no time for reading; after lectures my boy friends hurried me off to the movies. They were surprised to find that I did not even know the actors' names. I sat with them on sunny café terraces, I savored the pleasure of drifting along with the crowds, of having a drink, of being with a boy who looked deep into my eyes, held my hand, and then led me far away from those same crowds. We would walk slowly home. In the doorway he would draw me close and embrace me; I found out how pleasant it was to be kissed. I don't put names to these memories: Jean, Hubert, Jacques. They are common in the experiences of all young girls. In the evenings my diversions were more adult; I went to parties with my father. They were very mixed parties, and I was rather out of place, but I enjoyed myself, and the fact that I was so young seemed to amuse every-

one. At the end of the evening my father would drop
me at our flat, and then see his companion home. I
never heard him come in.

I do not want to give the impression that he was vain
about his love affairs, but he made no effort to hide
them from me, or to invent stories to explain the frequent presence at breakfast of a female friend, not even
when she later on became a temporary member of our
household. Besides I would soon have discovered the
nature of his relations with his "guests," and probably
he found it easier to be frank than to take the trouble
to deceive me, and thereby lose my confidence. The
result, however, was that I adopted a cynical attitude
toward love which, considering my age and experience,
should have meant happiness rather than mere sensation.
I was fond of repeating to myself sayings like Oscar
Wilde's:

"Sin is the only note of vivid color that persists in the
modern world."

I made this attitude my own with far more convic-
tion, I think, than if I had immediately put it into prac-
tice. I believed I could base my life on it, I forgot the
bad times, the up and downs, day-to-day happiness. I
visualized a life of degradation and moral turpitude as
my ideal.

Chapter 3

THE next morning I was awakened by a slanting ray of hot sunshine that flooded my bed and put an end to my strange and rather confused dreams. Still half asleep, I put my hand up to shield my face from the insistent heat, then gave it up. It was ten o'clock. I went down to the terrace in my pajamas and found Anne glancing through the newspapers. I noticed that she was lightly but perfectly made up; apparently she never allowed herself a real holiday from that. As she paid no attention to me, I sat down on the steps with a cup of coffee and an orange, enjoying the delicious morning. I bit the orange and let its sweet juice run into my mouth, then took a gulp of scalding black coffee and went back to the orange again. The sun warmed my hair and smoothed away the marks of the sheet on my skin. In five minutes I would go for a swim. Anne's voice made me jump.

"Cécile, aren't you eating anything?"

"I like just a drink in the morning."

"To look at all decent you ought to put on six pounds. Your cheeks are hollow and every rib shows. Do go in and get yourself some bread and butter!"

I begged her not to force me to eat, and she was explaining how important it was, when my father appeared in his luxurious, dotted silk dressing gown.

"What a charming spectacle," he said. "Two little girls sunning themselves and discussing bread and butter."

"Alas, there's only one little girl," said Anne gaily. "Remember I'm your age, my dear Raymond."

My father bent over her and took her hand.

"Still outspoken as ever!" he said tenderly, and I saw Anne's eyelids flutter as if she had received an unexpected caress.

I slipped away unnoticed. On the stairs I passed Elsa. She was obviously just out of bed, with swollen eyelids, pale lips, and her skin red and peeling from too much sun. I almost stopped her to tell her that Anne was already downstairs, her face trim and immaculate—that Anne would be careful to tan slowly and without burning. I thought to put her on her guard, but probably she would have taken it badly. She was twenty-nine, thirteen years younger than Anne, and that seemed to her a trump card.

I got my bathing suit and ran to the cove. To my surprise, Cyril was already there, sitting in his boat. He came to meet me looking serious, took my hands and led me toward the boat.

"I wanted to beg your pardon for yesterday," he said.

"It was my fault," I replied, wondering why he was so solemn.

"I'm very much annoyed with myself," he went on, pushing the boat into the water.

"There's no reason to be," I said lightly.

"But I am!"

I was already in the boat. He was standing in the water up to his knees, resting his hands on the gunwale as if it were the bar of a tribunal. I knew his face well enough to read his expression and I realized that he would not join me until he had said what was on his mind. It made me laugh to think that at the age of twenty-five he still could think of himself as a base seducer.

"Don't laugh," he said. "I really would have gone the whole way, yesterday afternoon. You have no protection against me. Look at the example your father and that woman set you! I might be the most awful cad for all you know."

I did not find him absurd. I saw he was kind, that he was on the verge of real love. I thought it would be nice for me to be in love with him, too. I put my arms around his neck and my cheek against his. He had broad shoulders; his body felt hard against mine.

"You're very sweet, Cyril," I murmured. "You shall be a brother to me."

He pressed his arms around me with an angry little

exclamation, and gently pulled me out of the boat. He lifted me up and held me close against him, my head on his shoulder. At that moment I loved him. In the morning light he was as golden, as soft, as gentle as myself, and he would protect me. As his lips touched mine we both began to tremble with pleasure; our kiss was untinged by shame or regret; it was merely a deep searching, interrupted every now and then by whispers. At last I broke away and swam toward the boat, which was drifting out. I dipped my face into the green water to refresh it. A feeling of wild happiness came over me.

At half-past eleven Cyril left, and my father and his two women appeared on the goat path. He was walking between them, offering his hand to each in turn to help them, with a charm and naturalness all his own. Anne was still wearing her beach coat. She removed it with complete unconcern while we all watched her, and lay down on the sand. She had a small waist and perfect legs, and, no doubt as the result of a lifetime of care and attention, her skin was almost without a blemish. Involuntarily I glanced at my father, raising an eyebrow of approval. To my great surprise he did not respond, but instead closed his eyes. Poor Elsa, whose skin was in a lamentable condition, was busy oiling herself. I did not think my father would stand her for another week. . . . Anne turned her head toward me.

"Cécile, why do you get up so early here? In Paris you stayed in bed until midday."

"I was studying then," I said. "That wore me out."

She did not smile. She smiled only when she felt like it, never out of politeness, like other people.

"How did you make out with your examinations?"

"Flunked!" I said, cheerfully. "Completely flunked."

"But you must pass in October, you absolutely *must*!"

"Why should she?" my father interrupted. "I never got any diploma and I manage to live very well."

"You had quite a fortune to start with," Anne reminded him.

"My daughter will always have a man to take care of her," said my father grandiloquently.

Elsa began to laugh, but stopped when she saw our three faces.

"Cécile will have to study during her vacation," said Anne, shutting her eyes to put an end to the conversation.

I gave my father a despairing look but he merely smiled sheepishly. I saw myself in front of an open page of Bergson, its black lines dancing before my eyes, while Cyril was waiting for me at the cove. The idea horrified me. I crept over to Anne and spoke to her in a low voice. She opened her eyes. I bent an anxious, pleading face toward her, drawing in my cheeks to look like an overworked intellectual.

"Anne," I said, "you're not going to make me do *that* —make me study in this heat. The rest is doing me so much good!"

She stared at me for a moment, then smiled mysteriously and turned her head away.

"I shall have to make you do *that*, even in this heat, as you say. You'll hold it against me for a day or two, if I know you, but you'll pass your exam."

"There are things one cannot be made to do," I said grimly.

Her only response was a superior smile, and I returned to my place on the beach full of foreboding. Elsa was chattering about various festivities taking place along the Riviera, but my father was not listening. From his place at the apex of the triangle formed by their bodies, he was gazing at Anne's upturned profile with a resolute stare that I recognized. His hand opened and closed on the sand with a gentle, regular, persistent movement. I ran down to the sea and plunged in, bemoaning the gay vacation we might have had. All the elements of a drama were to hand: a libertine, a demimondaine, and a strong-minded woman. I saw an exquisite pink and blue shell on the sea-bottom. I dove for it, and held it, smooth and hollow in my hand all the morning. I decided it was a lucky charm, and that I would keep it. I am surprised that I have not lost it, for I lose everything. Today it is still pink and warm as it lies in my palm, and makes me feel like crying.

Chapter 4

ANNE was extremely kind to Elsa during the following days. In spite of the numerous silly remarks that punctuated Elsa's conversation, Anne never gave vent to any of those sharp phrases which were her specialty, and which would have made poor Elsa ridiculous. I was most surprised, and began to admire Anne's forbearance and generosity, without realizing how subtle she was being. My father would soon have tired of cruel tactics, and he was now so filled with gratitude toward Anne that he could not do enough to please her. He used this gratitude as a means for drawing her, so to speak, into the family circle, suggesting constantly that I was partly Anne's responsibility, and in general behaving toward her as if she were a second mother to me. But I noticed that his every look and gesture betrayed a secret desire for her, a woman whom he had not possessed and whom he longed to enjoy. I had observed a similar gleam in Cyril's eye, and I hesitated between egging him on and running away. In this respect I must have been more susceptible than Anne, for her attitude to my father showed such reserve, such calm friendliness, that I was reassured. I began to believe that I had been mistaken that first day. I was not aware that her engaging frankness was just what excited my father. And then there were her silences, apparently so artless, so sensitive, such a contrast to Elsa's incessant chatter, that it was light and shade. Poor Elsa! She had really no suspicion whatsoever, and, although still suffering from sunburn, remained her usual talkative and exuberant self.

A day came, however, when she must have intercepted a look of my father's and drawn her own conclusions from it. Before lunch I saw her whispering into his ear. For a moment he seemed rather put out, but then he nodded and smiled. After coffee, Elsa walked over to the door, turned around, and struck a languorous, movie-star pose. In her voice was ten years of French coquetry:

"Are you coming, Raymond?"

My father got up, almost blushing, and muttered something about the good to be derived from a nap after a meal as he followed Elsa. Anne had not moved. Her cigarette was smoldering between her fingers. I felt I ought to say something:

"People say that a siesta is restful, but I think it can be quite the reverse . . . "

I stopped short, conscious that my words were equivocal.

"That's enough," said Anne dryly.

There was nothing equivocal about *her* tone. She had, of course, found my remark in bad taste but when I looked at her I saw that she had kept herself calm and composed only with an effort. Perhaps at that very moment she was passionately jealous of Elsa. While I was wondering how I could console her, a cynical idea occurred to me. Cynicism always enchanted me; gave me a delightful feeling of self-assurance and self-approbation. I could not keep it back.

"I imagine that with Elsa's sunburn that kind of siesta can't be much fun for either of them."

I would have done better to keep quiet.

"I detest that kind of remark. At your age it's worse than stupid. It's painful."

I responded angrily: "I only said it as a joke, you know. I'm sure they are really quite happy."

She turned to me with an outraged expression, and I at once apologized. She closed her eyes and began to speak in a low, patient voice.

"Your idea of love is rather primitive. Love is not a series of sensations, each one independent of the others ..."

I realized that every time I had fallen in love it had been just like that: a sudden emotion, aroused by a face, a gesture or a kiss, ... thrilling moments, without coherence, was all I remembered.

"It is something different," said Anne. "There are such things as lasting affection, sweetness, a need ... but I suppose you cannot understand."

She dismissed me with a gesture and took up a newspaper. If only she had been angry instead of resigned to my lack of sentiment. All the same I felt she was right—that I was governed by my instincts like an animal, swayed this way and that by other people, that I was shallow and weak. I despised myself, and it was a horribly painful sensation, all the more since I was not used to self-criticism. I went up to my room in a daze. Lying in bed on my warm sheet I thought of Anne's words: "It is something different, it's a need." Had I ever *needed* anyone?

The next fortnight is rather vague in my memory because I deliberately shut my eyes to any threat to our security, but the rest of the vacation stands out clearly because of the role I chose to play in it.

To go back to those first three weeks, three happy weeks on the whole: when was it my father first looked openly at Anne's mouth? Was it the day he reproached her for her aloofness, while pretending to laugh at it? Or the time he solemnly compared her subtlety with Elsa's near-imbecility? My peace of mind was based on the stupid idea that they had known each other for fifteen years, and that if they had been going to fall in love, they would have done so earlier. And I thought also that if it had to happen, the affair would last at the most three months, and Anne would be left with her memories and perhaps a slight feeling of humiliation. Yet all the time I knew in my heart that Anne was not a woman who could be lightly forsaken.

But Cyril was there and filled my thoughts. In the evenings he and I often drove to Saint Tropez and danced in various night clubs to the soft music of a clarinet. At those moments we felt we were madly in love, but by the next morning it was all forgotten. During the day we went sailing. My father sometimes came with us. He thought well of Cyril, especially since Cyril had allowed him to win a swimming race.

He called Cyril "my boy," and Cyril called him "Sir." But I sometimes wondered which of the two was the adult.

One afternoon we went to have tea with Cyril's mother, a quiet smiling old lady who spoke to us of her problems as a widow and mother. My father sympathized with her, looking toward Anne for aid, and paid the old lady innumerable compliments. I must say he never minded giving his time! Anne looked on at the spectacle with an amiable smile, and afterwards said she thought Cyril's mother was charming. I broke into imprecations against old ladies of that sort. Anne and my father laughed at me, which made me furious.

"Don't you realize how pleased she is with herself?" I insisted. "That she pats herself on the back because she feels she has done her duty and . . . "

"But it is true," said Anne. "She has done her duty as a wife and mother, as they say."

"But how about her duty as a mistress?" I asked.

"I don't like vulgarities," Anne said, "even if witty."

"But I'm not trying to be witty. She married the way everyone marries, from desire, or because it's the thing to do. She had a baby—you know where babies come from?"

"Probably not as well as you do," Anne said with irony. "But I have an idea."

"She brought up her child. She probably begrudged herself the bother of a love affair. She had a life like millions of other wives, and she is proud of it, you understand. She had the position of a young, middle-class wife and mother, and she did nothing to jeopardize it. She's pleased with herself for what she hasn't done, not for having accomplished anything."

"That makes no sense," said my father.

"It's like a bird admiring itself," I cried. "She says to herself: 'I did my duty' and she has done nothing. If, with her background, she had become a girl of the streets, that would be worth praising."

"Your ideas are fashionable, but you don't know what you are talking about," Anne said.

She was probably right. At the time, I believed what I said but I must admit that I was only repeating what I had heard. Nevertheless my life and my father's followed my ideas and Anne hurt my feelings by despising them. One can be just as much attached to futilities as to anything else. Anne did not consider me a person with brains. I felt an ardent desire to prove her wrong. I had no idea the opportunity would occur so soon, nor that I would be able to seize it. Anyhow it was quite likely that in a month's time I would have entirely different opinions on any given subject. What more could have been expected of me?

Chapter 5

AND then one day things came to a head. In the morning my father said he would like to go to Cannes that evening to dance at the casino, and perhaps gamble as well. I remember how pleased Elsa was. In the familiar casino atmosphere she hoped to resume her role of *femme fatale,* which had been dimmed of late by her sunburn and our semi-isolation. Contrary to my expectation, Anne did not oppose our plans. She even seemed quite pleased. As soon as dinner was over I went up to my room to put on an evening dress, as it happened the only one I possessed. It had been chosen by my father, and was made of an exotic material, probably too exotic for a girl of my age. But my father, either from inclination or habit, liked to have me look sophisticated. I found him downstairs, handsome in a new dinner jacket, and I put my arms around his neck.

"You're the best-looking man I know."

"Except Cyril," he answered insincerely. "And as for you, you're the prettiest girl I know."

"After Elsa and Anne," I replied, also without believing it.

"Since they're not down yet, and have the cheek to keep me waiting, come and dance with your rheumaticky old father!"

Once again I felt the thrill that always preceded our evenings out together. He really had nothing of an old father about him! While dancing I inhaled his familiar odor: a mixture of eau de cologne, warmth and tobacco. He danced slowly, with half-closed eyes, a happy, irrepressible little smile, like my own, on his lips.

"You must teach me the bebop sometime," he said, forgetting his talk of rheumatism.

He stopped dancing to greet Elsa with polite flattery. She came slowly down the stairs in her green dress, a conventional smile on her face, her casino smile. She had made the most of her sun-dried hair and scorched skin, but the result was praiseworthy rather than brilliant. Fortunately she seemed unaware of it.

"Are we off?"

"Anne's not down yet," I remarked.

"Go up and see if she's ready," said my father. "It will be midnight before we get to Cannes."

I ran up the stairs, getting somewhat entangled with my long skirt, and knocked at Anne's door. She called to me to come in, but I stopped on the threshold. She was wearing a gray dress, a very special gray, almost white, which when it caught the light, looked like the sea at dawn. She seemed to me the personification of mature charm. "Oh, Anne, what a magnificent dress!" I said.

She smiled into the mirror as one smiles at a person to whom one is saying good-by.

"This gray *is* a success," she said.

"*You* are a success!" I exclaimed.

She pinched my ear. Her dark-blue eyes lit up with a smile.

"You're a dear child even though you can be irritating at times."

She went out ahead of me without a glance at my dress. In a way I was relieved, but all the same it was mortifying. I followed her down the stairs and I saw my father coming to meet her. He stopped at the bottom, his foot on the first step, his face raised. Elsa was looking on. I remember the scene perfectly. First of all, in front of me, Anne's golden neck and perfect shoulders, a little lower down my father's fascinated face and extended hand, and, off in the background, Elsa's silhouette.

"Anne, you are wonderful!" said my father.

She smiled as she passed him and took her coat.

"Shall we meet at the casino? Cécile, will you come with me?"

She let me drive. At night the road appeared so beautiful that I drove slowly. Anne was silent; she did not even seem to notice the noisy radio. When my father's car passed us at a curve she remained unmoved. I felt I was out of the race, watching a performance in which I could not interfere.

At the casino my father saw to it that we soon lost sight of each other. I found myself at the bar with Elsa and one of her acquaintances, a half-tipsy South American. He was connected with the theater and had such a passionate love for it that even in his drunken condition he could make it interesting. I spent an agreeable hour with him, but Elsa was bored. She liked to hear big names mentioned, but the theater was not her world. Suddenly she asked me where my father was, as if I had some way of knowing. She then left us. The South American seemed put out for a moment, but another whisky set him up again. My mind was a blank. I was quite lightheaded, for I had been drinking with him out of politeness. It became still funnier when he wanted to dance. I was forced to hold him up, and to extricate my feet from under his, which required a lot of agility. We laughed so much that when Elsa tapped me on the shoulder and I saw her Cassandra-like expression, I felt like telling her to go to the devil.

"I can't find them," she said.

She looked utterly distraught. Her powder had worn off, leaving her skin shiny, and her features were drawn. She was a pitiful sight. I suddenly felt very angry with my father; he was being incredibly rude.

"Ah, I know where they are," I said smiling as if everything was as usual and she need have no anxiety. "I'll soon be back."

Deprived of my support, the South American fell in

Elsa's arms and seemed quite content there. I reflected somewhat sadly that she was more generously built than I, and I could not hold this against her.

The casino was large, and I went all round it twice without any success. I scanned the terrace and at last thought of the car. It took me some time to find it in the park. They were inside. I approached from behind and saw them through the rear window. Their profiles were very close together, very serious and strangely beautiful in the lamplight. They were facing each other and must have been talking in low tones for I saw their lips move. I would have liked to go away but the thought of Elsa made me open the door. My father had his hand on Anne's arm, and they scarcely noticed me.

"Are you having a good time?" I asked politely.

"What is the matter?" said my father irritably. "What are you doing here?"

"And you? Elsa has been looking for you everywhere for the past hour."

Anne turned her head toward me slowly and reluctantly.

"We're going home. Tell her I was tired and your father had to drive me back. When you've had enough fun, drive my car home."

I was trembling with indignation and could hardly speak.

"Had fun enough? But you don't realize what you're doing! It's disgusting!"

"What is disgusting?" asked my father. astonished.

"You take a red-headed girl to the seashore, expose her to the hot sun which she can't stand, and when her skin has all peeled, you abandon her. It's too easy! What on earth shall I say to Elsa?"

Anne turned to him with an air of weariness. He smiled at her, obviously not listening to me. My exasperation knew no bounds.

"I shall tell Elsa that my father has found someone else to sleep with, and that she can call again another time. Is that right?"

My father's exclamation and Anne's slap were simultaneous. I hurriedly withdrew my head from the car door. She had hurt me.

"Apologize at once!" said my father.

I stood motionless and silent with my thoughts in a whirl. Telling retorts always occur to me too late.

"Come here!" said Anne.

She did not sound angry, so I went closer. She put her hand against my cheek and spoke slowly and gently as if I were rather dumb.

"Don't be naughty. I'm very sorry about Elsa, but you are tactful enough to handle her right. Tomorrow we'll discuss it all. Did I hurt you very much?"

"Not at all," I said politely. Her sudden gentleness after my intemperate rage made me want to burst into tears. I watched them drive away, feeling completely deflated. My only consolation was the thought of the tactfulness she had imputed to me.

I walked slowly back to the casino where I found

Elsa with the South American clinging to her arm.

"Anne wasn't well," I said in an offhand manner. "Papa had to take her home. How about a drink?"

She looked at me without answering. I tried to find a more convincing explanation.

"She was awfully sick," I said. "It was ghastly, her dress is ruined." This detail seemed to make my story more plausible, but Elsa began to weep quietly and sadly. I did not know what to do.

"Oh, Cécile, we were all so happy!" she said and her sobs redoubled in intensity. The South American began to cry, repeating, "We were so happy, so happy!" At that moment I heartily detested Anne and my father. I would have done anything to stop Elsa from crying, her mascara from running, and the South American from howling.

"Nothing is settled yet, Elsa; come home with me now!"

"No! I'll come and get my suitcase later," she sobbed. 'Good-by! We got on well together, didn't we, Cécile?"

We had never talked of anything but clothes or the weather, but still it seemed to me that I was losing an old friend. I quickly turned away and ran to the car.

Chapter 6

THE following morning I was wretched, probably because of the whisky I had drunk the night before. I awoke in my darkened room to find myself lying across my bed—my tongue heavy, my limbs unbearably damp and sticky. A single ray of sunshine filtered through the slats of the shutters and I could see a million motes dancing in it. I felt no desire to get up, nor to stay in bed. I wondered how Anne and my father would take it if Elsa were to turn up that morning. I forced myself to think of them in order to be able to get out of bed. At last I managed to stand up on my cool, tiled floor. I was giddy and aching.

The mirror reflected a sad sight. I leaned against it and peered at those dilated eyes and dry lips, the face of a stranger. Was that my face? If I was weak and cowardly, could it be because of those lips, the particular shape of my body, these odious, arbitrary physical limitations? And if I were limited, why had I only now become aware of it? I occupied myself by detesting my reflection, hating that wolf-like face, hollow and worn by debauchery. I repeated the word "debauchery" looking into my eyes in the mirror. And then suddenly

I saw myself smile. What a great debauch! A few miserable drinks, a slap in the face, and some tears! I brushed my teeth and went downstairs.

My father and Anne were already on the terrace, sitting beside each other at their breakfast tray. I sat down opposite them, muttering a "good morning." A feeling of shyness made me keep my eyes lowered, but after a time, as they remained silent, I was forced to look at them. Anne appeared tired, the only sign of a night of love. They were both smiling happily, and I was very much impressed, for happiness has always seemed to me a great achievement.

"Did you sleep well?" asked my father.

"Not too badly," I replied. "I drank a lot of whisky last night."

I poured out a cup of coffee, but after the first sip I quickly put it down. Their silence had an expectant quality that made me feel uneasy. I was too tired to bear it for long.

"What's the matter? You look so mysterious."

My father lighted a cigarette, making an obvious effort to seem unconcerned, and for once in her life Anne seemed embarrassed.

"I would like to ask you something," she said at last.

"You want me to take another message to Elsa?" I said, imagining the worst.

She turned toward my father. "Your father and I want to get married," she said.

I stared first at her, then at my father. I half expected

some sign from him, perhaps a wink, which, though I might have found it shocking, would have reassured me. But he was looking down at his hands. I said to myself, "It can't be possible!" But I already knew it was true.

"What a good idea," I said to gain time.

I could not understand how my father, who had always set himself so obstinately against marriage and its chains, could have decided on it in a single night. We were about to lose our independence. I could visualize our future family life, a life newly balanced by Anne's intelligence and refinement—the kind of life I had envied her. We would have clever, tactful friends, and quiet pleasant evenings. . . . I found myself despising noisy dinners, South Americans, and girls like Elsa. I felt proud and superior.

"It's a very, very good idea," I repeated, and I smiled at them.

"I knew you'd be pleased, my pet," said my father.

He was relaxed and delighted. Anne's face, subtly changed by love, seemed gentler, making her more accessible than she had ever been before.

"Come here, my pet," said my father, and holding out his hands, he drew me close to them both. I was half-kneeling in front of them, while they stroked my hair and looked at me tenderly. But I could not keep from thinking that although my life was perhaps at that very moment changing its whole course, I was in reality nothing more than a kitten to them, an affectionate little animal. I felt them above me, united by a past and a future, by ties that I did not know and which could not hold me. But I deliberately closed my eyes and went on playing my part, laying my head on their knees and laughing. For was I not happy? Anne was all right, there was nothing the least mean about her. She would guide me, relieve me of responsibility, and be at hand whenever I might need her. She would make both my father and me into paragons of virtue.

My father went to get a bottle of champagne. My spirits sank. He was happy, which was the chief thing, but I had so often seen him happy on account of a woman.

"I was rather frightened of you," said Anne.

"Why?" I asked. Her words suggested that a veto from me could have stopped their marriage.

"I was afraid of your being frightened of me," she said laughing.

I began to laugh, too, because actually I was a little scared of her. She wanted me to understand that she knew it, and that I did not need to fear her.

"Does the marriage of two old people like ourselves seem ridiculous to you?"

"You're not old," I said emphatically, as my father came prancing back with a bottle in his hand.

He sat down next to Anne and put an arm around her shoulders. She turned toward him in a way that made me lower my eyes. She was no doubt marrying him for just that; for his laughter, for the firm reassurance of his arm, for his vitality, his warmth. At forty there could be the fear of solitude, or perhaps a final upsurge of the senses. . . . I had never thought of Anne as a woman, but as a personality. I had seen her as a self-assured, elegant, and clever person, but never as weak or sensual. I quite understood that my father felt proud—the proud, reserved Anne Larsen was going to marry him. But did he love her, and if so, was he capable of loving her for long? Was there any difference between this new feeling for her and the feeling he had had for Elsa? The sun was making my head spin, and I shut my eyes. We were all three on the terrace, full of unspoken thoughts, of secret fears, and of happiness.

Elsa did not come back during this time. A week flew by, seven happy, companionable days—and then things changed. While it lasted we made detailed plans for redecorating our Paris flat, and discussed a routine for our life which my father and I took pleasure in elaborating with the blind obstinancy of those who have never had any use for routines. Did he and I ever believe in them for one moment? Did my father really think it possible to have lunch every day at the same place at twelve-thirty sharp, to have dinner at home and spend a quiet evening? Nevertheless he cheerfully prepared to abandon Bohemianism, and began to preach order, to extol the joys of a cultivated, well-organized, bourgeois existence. No doubt for him, as for me, all these plans were just castles in the air.

How well I remember that week! Anne was relaxed, trusting, and very sweet; my father loved her. I saw them coming down in the mornings, leaning on each other, laughing gaily, with shadows under their eyes, and I swear that I should have liked nothing better than that this happiness should last all their lives. In the evening we often drank an apéritif sitting on the terrace of some seaside café. Everywhere we went we were taken for a happy, normal family, and I, who was used to going out alone with my father and seeing the knowing smiles, the malicious or pitying glances, was delighted to play a role more suitable to my age. They were to be married on our return to Paris.

Poor Cyril had witnessed the transformation in our life with a certain amazement, but he was comforted by the thought that this time it would be legalized. We still went sailing together and kissed whenever we felt inclined. But sometimes as he pressed his lips on mine I thought of Anne's face as I saw it every morning, with its softened contours. I recalled the happy ease, the languid grace that love imparted to her movements, and I envied her. Kisses alone can cease to satisfy, and no doubt if Cyril had not been so fond of me, I would have become his mistress that very week.

At six o'clock , on our return from the islands, Cyril would pull the boat onto the sand. We would go up to the house through the pine woods, single file, pretending we were Indians. Or we would run handicap races to warm ourselves up. He always caught me before we reached the house and would spring on me with a shout of victory, rolling me on the pine needles, pinning my arms down and kissing me. I can still remember the taste of those breath-taking kisses, and hear Cyril's heart beating against mine in rhythm with the soft thud of the surf on the beach. One—two—three, his heart pounded out, and one—two—three sounded the waves. Then gradually, as he regained his breath, his kisses would become more urgent, the sound of the sea would grow dim and give way to the pulse beating in my ears.

One evening Anne's voice separated us. Cyril was lying against me. We were half-naked in the red glow of the sunset, and I can understand that Anne might have been deceived by what she saw. She called to me sharply.

Cyril bounded to his feet, naturally somewhat abashed. Keeping my eyes on Anne, I in turn slowly got up. She faced Cyril, and looking right through him, spoke in a quiet voice:

"I don't wish to see you again."

He made no reply, but bent over and kissed my shoulder before departing. I felt surprised and touched, as if his gesture were a sort of pledge. Anne was staring at me with the same grave, detached look, as though she were thinking of something else. Her manner infuriated me. If she were so deep in thought why speak at all? I went up to her, politely pretending to be embarrassed. At last she seemed to notice me and abstractedly removed a pine needle from my neck. I saw her face assume its beautiful mask of disdain, that expression of weariness and superiority which became

her so well, and which always frightened me a little.
"You should realize that such diversions usually end
up in a hospital."

She stood there looking straight at me as she spoke,
and I was horribly ashamed. She was one of those women who can stand perfectly still while they talk. I
always needed the support of a chair, or some object to
hold, like a cigarette, or the distraction of swinging one
leg over the other and watching it move.

"Don't exaggerate," I said with a smile. "I was only
kissing Cyril, and that won't lead me to any hospital."

"Please don't see him again," she said, as if she did not
believe me. "And don't protest. You are only seventeen
and I feel a certain responsibility for you now. I'm not
going to let you ruin your life. In any case you have
studying to do, and that will take up your afternoons."

She turned her back on me and walked toward the
house in her nonchalant way. Shock rooted me to the
spot. She had meant every word. What was the use of
arguments or denials when she would receive them with
the sort of indifference that was worse than contempt,
as if I did not even exist, as if I were something to be
squashed underfoot, and not myself, Cécile, whom she
had always known. My only hope now was my father.
Surely he would say as usual: "Well now, what boy is
it this time? I hope he's at least handsome and healthy.
But keep away from the wolves, my girl!" If he did not
react like this, my vacation would be ruined.

Dinner was a nightmare. Not for a moment had Anne

intimated to me that she would not be a tattle-tale and tell my father about it if I would promise to study. It was not in her nature to bargain. In a way I approved of her as she was, but still I would have liked some action from her that would give me a chance to despise her. As usual she avoided a false move, and it was only when we had finished our soup that she seemed to remember the incident.

"I do wish you'd give your daughter some advice, Raymond. I came across her in the woods with Cyril this evening, and they seemed to be going rather far."

My father, poor man, tried to pass the whole thing off as a joke.

"What's that you say? What were they up to?"

"He was kissing me," I said, "and Anne thought . . . "

"I never thought anything at all," she interrupted. "But it might be a good idea for her to stop seeing him for a time and to work at her philosophy instead."

"Oh, the poor little thing!" said my father. "After all, Cyril's a nice boy, isn't he?"

"And Cécile is a nice girl," said Anne. "That's why I should be heartbroken if anything should happen to her, and it seems to me inevitable that it will if she continues to have such complete freedom. She and Cyril are constantly together and both are completely idle. So what can one expect? Don't you agree?"

At her last words I lifted my eyes and my father lowered his, very embarrassed.

"You are probably right," he said. "After all, you

ought to do some work, Cécile. You surely don't want to fail in philosophy and have to take it again?"

"What do you think I care?" I answered sharply.

He glanced at me and then turned away. I was bewildered. I realized that carelessness can govern our lives, but it does not provide us with any arguments in its defense.

"Listen," said Anne, taking my hand across the table. "Won't you drop your role of a wood nymph and become a good schoolgirl for just one month? Would that be so hard?"

They both looked at me, smiling affectionately. Seen in that light, the argument was obvious. I gently withdrew my hand.

"Yes, very hard," I said so softly that they did not hear it, or did not want to.

The following morning I came across a paragraph from Bergson. It took me several minutes to understand it:

"Whatever irrelevance one may at first find between the cause and the effects, and although a rule of guidance towards an assertion concerning the root of things may be far distant, it is always in a contact with the generative force of life that one is able to extract the power to love humanity."

I repeated the paragraph, quietly at first, so as not to get agitated, then in a louder voice. I held my head in my hands and looked at the words intently. At last I understood it, but I felt as cold and impotent as when I had read it the first time. I simply could not go on with my reading. With the best will in the world I applied myself to the next lines, but suddenly something arose in me like a storm and threw me onto the bed. I thought of Cyril waiting for me down in the golden cove, of the gently swaying boat, of the taste of our kisses, and I I thought of Anne, but in a way that made me sit up on my bed with a fast-beating heart, telling myself that I was stupid, monstrous, nothing but a lazy, spoiled child, and had no right to have such thoughts. But just the same, in spite of myself, I went on thinking that she was a danger to me, and that I must get rid of her. I thought of the dinner I had endured with clenched teeth, tortured by a feeling of resentment for which I despised and ridiculed myself.

Yes, it was this I held against Anne: she kept me from liking myself. I, who was naturally meant for happiness and gaiety, had been forced by her into self-criticism and a guilty conscience. Unaccustomed to introspection, I was completely lost. And what good did she do me? I took stock: she wanted my father; she had got him. She would gradually turn us into the husband and step-daughter of Anne Larsen, that is to say, she would turn us into two civilized, well-behaved and contented persons. For she would certainly be good to us. How easily —unstable and irresponsible as we were—we would yield to her influence, and be fitted into the attractive framework of her orderly plan of living. She was much too efficient. Already my father was separated from me. I was hurt by his embarrassed face, turning away from me at the table. Tears came into my eyes at the thought of the jokes we used to have together, our gay laughter as we drove home at dawn through the deserted streets of Paris. All that was over. In my turn I would be influenced, readjusted, remodeled by Anne. I would not even mind it, she would handle me with such intelligence, humor and sweetness. I wouldn't be able to resist her. In six months I should no longer even want to.

At all costs I must save myself, regain my father and our former life. How infinitely charming those two years with him now seemed, those gay times I was so ready to give up just the other day . . . the freedom to think for myself, even to think wrongly or not at all, the freedom to choose my own life, to choose myself. I cannot say I wanted to "be myself," for I knew I was still soft clay. But I refused to be molded.

I realize that some people might find complicated motives for this revolt in me. Some might endow me with startling complexes: such as an incestuous love for my father, or a morbid passion for Anne. But I know the true reasons were the heat, Bergson and Cyril, or rather Cyril's absence. My thoughts went on all the afternoon. I was in a most unpleasant mood, brought on by the discovery that we were entirely at Anne's mercy. I was not used to reflection, and it made me irritable. At dinner, as in the morning, I did not open my mouth. My father finally attempted a little teasing:

"What I like about youth is its spontaneity, its gay conversation."

I was trembling with rage. It was true that he loved youth; and with whom could I have talked if not with him? We had discussed everything together: love, death, music. Now he himself had silenced me, abandoned me. Looking at him I thought: "You don't love me any more, you have betrayed me!" I tried to make him understand without words how desperate I was. I gave myself up completely to hysteria. Suddenly he seemed to sense it; perhaps he understood that the time for joking was past, and that our relationship was in danger. I saw him stiffen, and he seemed about to speak to me. Anne turned to me:

"You don't look well. I'm sorry now I made you study."

I did not reply. I felt too disgusted that I had got myself into a state which I could no longer control. We had finished dinner. On the terrace, in the rectangle of light projected from the dining-room window, I saw Anne's long nervous hand reach out to find my father's. I thought of Cyril. I would have liked him to take me in his arms on that terrace, flooded with moonlight and the noise of the crickets. I would have liked to be caressed, consoled, reconciled with myself. My father and Anne were silent. They had a night of love to look forward to; I had Bergson. I tried to cry, to feel sorry for myself, but in vain. Already I was sorry for Anne, as if I were certain that I would conquer her.

PART TWO

Chapter 1

HOW clearly I remember everything from that moment on! I acquired an added awareness of other people and of myself. An unthinking, easy egoism had been natural to me. I had always lived like this. But the last few days had upset me deeply, forcing me to reflect, to look at myself with a critical eye. I endured all the pangs of introspection, and still couldn't become reconciled with myself. "These feelings," I thought, "these feelings about Anne are mean and stupid; this desire to separate her from my father is vicious." But after all, why was I so hard on myself? Wasn't I free to judge what happened? For the first time in my life my "self" seemed to be split, and I discovered opposing forces within that shocked me. I found good excuses, I whispered them to myself, trying to be honest, and suddenly another "me" rose up which answered all my arguments, saying that I was fooling myself with them, although they had all the appearance of truth. But truly, wasn't it this other "me" who was wrong? Wasn't this clear-headedness my worst mistake? Up in my room I reasoned with myself for hours on end in an attempt to discover whether the

fear and hostility which Anne inspired in me were justi-
fied, or if I was merely a silly, spoiled, selfish girl pretending to be adult.

In the meantime I grew thinner every day. On the
beach I did nothing but sleep, and at mealtimes I main-
tained a strained silence that finally made the others
uneasy.

And all the time I watched Anne. At dinner I would
say to myself, "Everything she does shows how much
she loves him. Could anyone be more in love? How can
I be angry with her when she smiles at me with that
worried look in her eyes?" But then she would say,
"When we get back home to Paris, Raymond . . . " And
the thought that she was going to share our life and
interfere with us would anger me again. Again she
seemed calculating and cold. I thought: "She is cold,
we are warm-hearted. She is dictatorial, we are easy-
going. She is standoffish; other people don't interest
her though we love them. She is reserved; we are gay.
Here we are, the two of us, and she will glide in between
us quietly. She will warm herself at our fire and gradually absorb our carefree warmth. She will have us in her
coils, like a beautiful serpent," I repeated, "just like a
beautiful serpent." Then Anne passed me the bread,
and suddenly I came to my senses. "But I'm crazy," I
thought. "That's Anne, your friend who was so kind
to you, who is so clever. Her aloofness is a mere habit,
there's nothing calculated about it. Her reserve is just
to shield her from countless sordid things in life. It's

a sign of nobility. A beautiful serpent . . . " I felt myself turn pale with shame. I looked at her, silently imploring her forgiveness. At times she noticed my expression and a shadow of surprise and concern would cloud her face and make her break off in the middle of a sentence. Then her eyes would turn instinctively to my father; but his glance never showed anything but admiration or desire. He did not understand the cause of her disquiet. Little by little I made the atmosphere unbearable, and I detested myself for it.

My father suffered as much as his nature permitted, that is to say, hardly at all, for he was mad about Anne, intensely proud and happy, and nothing else existed for him. However, one day when I was dozing on the beach after my morning swim, he sat down next to me and looked at me closely. I felt his eyes upon me, and with my air of false gaiety that was fast becoming a habit, I was about to ask him to come in for a swim when he put his hand on my head and called to Anne in a doleful voice:

"Come over here and have a look at this little creature. She's as thin as a rail. If this is the effect studying has on her, she'll have to give it up!"

He thought that would settle everything, and no doubt it would have done so ten days earlier. But by now I was too deeply immersed in complications, and the hours set aside for work in the afternoons no longer bothered me, especially as I had not opened a book since Bergson.

Anne came up to us. I remained lying face down on the sand, listening to the muffled sound of her footsteps. She sat on my other side.

"It certainly doesn't seem to agree with her," she said. "But if she really did some work instead of walking up and down in her room . . . "

I had turned around and was looking at them. How did she know that I was not studying? Perhaps she could even read my thoughts? I thought her capable of anything. It frightened me. I protested.

"I don't walk up and down in my room!"

"Are you lonesome for that boy?" asked my father.

"No!"

This was not quite true, but I certainly had had no time to think of Cyril.

"But still, you're not well," said my father firmly. "Anne, look at her. She looks like a chicken that has been plucked and put to roast in the sun."

"Cécile, dear," said Anne, "try to pull yourself together. Do just a little work and eat a great deal. That exam *is* important . . . "

"I don't care a hang about the exam!" I cried. "Can't you understand? I just don't care!"

I looked straight at her, despairingly, so that she should realize that something more serious than an exam was at stake. I longed for her to ask me, "Well, what *is* the matter?" and to ply me with questions, force me to tell her everything. Then I would be won over and she could do anything she liked with me, and I should no longer be in torment. She looked at me attentively. I could see the deep blue of her eyes darken with concentration and reproach. Then I understood that it would never occur to her to ply me with questions and so deliver me from myself, because even if the thought had entered her head, her code of behavior would have forbidden it. And I saw, too, that she had no idea of the tumult within me. Or even if she did, I thought, she would have withdrawn in disdain and disapproval, which was exactly what I deserved! Anne always gave everything its exact value; that is why I could never come to an understanding with her.

I dropped back onto the sand and laid my cheek against its soft warmth. I sighed deeply and began to tremble. I could feel Anne's hand, tranquil and steady, on the back of my neck, holding me still for a moment, just long enough to stop my nervous tremor. "Don't complicate life for yourself," she said. "You've always been so contented and lively, so thoughtless. And here you are now, sad and introspective. It doesn't suit you."

"I know," I answered. "I'm just a thoughtless, healthy child, gay and silly!"

"Come and have lunch," she said.

My father had moved away from us; he hated that sort of discussion. On the way back he took my hand and held it. His hand was firm and comforting; it had dried my tears after my first disappointment in love, it had closed over mine in moments of peace and perfect happiness, it had stealthily pressed mine at times when

we were misbehaving, or laughing riotously. I thought
of his hand on the steering wheel, or holding the door
keys at night and searching in vain for the lock; his
hand on a woman's shoulder, or holding a cigarette—
the hand that could do nothing more for me. I gave it
a hard squeeze. Turning toward me, he smiled.

Chapter 2

TWO days went by. I went around in circles, wearing myself out, but I could not free myself from the haunting thought that Anne was about to wreck our lives. I did not try to see Cyril. He could have comforted me and made me happier, but that was not what I wanted. I even got a certain satisfaction from asking myself unanswerable questions, by reminding myself of days gone by, and dreading those to come. It was very hot. I kept my room in semidarkness with the shutters closed, but even so the air was unbearably heavy and damp. I lay on my bed staring at the ceiling, moving only to search for a cooler place on the sheet. I could not sleep. Frequently I played records on the phonograph at the foot of my bed. I chose slow rhythms, without a melody. I smoked a good deal and felt decadent, which gave me pleasure. But I was not deluded by this game of pretense: I was sad and bewildered.

One afternoon the maid knocked at my door and announced with an air of mystery: "Someone's downstairs." I at once thought of Cyril and went down. It was not Cyril, but Elsa. She greeted me effusively.

Looking at her, I was astonished at her new beauty. She was marvelously tanned at last, evenly and smoothly, and was carefully made up and brilliantly youthful.

"I've come to get my suitcase," she explained. "Juan bought me a few dresses, but not enough, and I need my things."

I wondered for a moment who Juan could be, but did not inquire further. I was pleased Elsa had come back. She brought with her the aura of a kept woman, of bars, of gay evenings, which reminded me of happier days. I told her how glad I was to see her again, and she assured me that we had always got on so well together because we had common interests. I suppressed a slight shudder and suggested that we should go up to my room to avoid meeting Anne and my father. When I mentioned my father her head jerked involuntarily and I wondered whether she was still in love with him, in spite of Juan and the dresses. I also thought that three weeks before I would not have noticed that movement of her head.

In my room I listened while she described in glowing terms her smart and giddy life in the fashionable places along the Riviera. A strange confusion of thoughts went through my head, partly suggested by her improved appearance. At last she stopped talking, perhaps because I was silent. She took a few steps across the room, and without turning round, asked in an offhand way, "Is Raymond happy?" In a moment I realized what I must say to her.

" 'Happy' is saying too much. Anne doesn't give him a chance to think he isn't happy. She is very clever."

"Very!" sighed Elsa.

"You'll never guess what she's persuaded him to do! She's going to marry him . . . "

Elsa turned a horrified face toward me.

"Marry him? Raymond actually wants to get *married*?"

"Yes," I answered. "Raymond is going to be married."

A sudden desire to laugh caught me by the throat. My hands were shaking. Elsa seemed prostrated, almost as if I had struck her. I must not let her entertain the idea that he had reached the age when marriage was suitable, that he could not be expected to spend the rest of his life with demimondaines. I leaned forward and lowered my voice to make a stronger impression on her.

"It simply mustn't happen, Elsa. He's suffering already. It's an impossible state of affairs, as you can very well imagine."

"Yes," she said. She seemed fascinated by my words.

"You're just the person I've been waiting for," I went on. "Because you are the only one who is a match for Anne. You alone are up to her standard."

She seemed to swallow the bait. "But if he's marrying her it must be because he loves her!" she objected.

"But look here, Elsa, it's you he loves! Don't try to tell me you don't know it."

She blinked her eyelids, and turned away to hide the

pleasure and the hope my words had given her. I was in a kind of hypnotic state, but I knew just what I should say to her.

"Don't you see? Anne kept harping on the bliss of married life, and all that, and in the end she caught him."

I was surprised at my own words. For even though I had expressed myself somewhat crudely, that was indeed what I thought.

"If they get married, our three lives will be ruined, Elsa! My father must be protected. He's nothing but a big baby."

I repeated "a big baby" with stronger emphasis. It occurred to me that I might be overdoing my melodrama, but then I saw Elsa's beautiful green eyes fill with pity, and I wound up, as in a litany:

"Help me, Elsa! Give me aid! For your own sake! For the sake of my father! And for the love you bear each other!"

I added *sotto voce*: "And for the sake of John Chinaman!"

"But what can I *do*?" pleaded Elsa. "There seems no way out!"

"If you think there's no way out, then forget about it," I sadly said.

"What a bitch she is!" murmured Elsa.

"You've hit the nail on the head," I said, turning away to hide my satisfaction.

Elsa visibly brightened up. Her ideas poured forth. She had been jilted, she said, and now she was going to show that adventuress just what she, Elsa Mackenbourg, could do. And of course my father loved her; she had always known he loved her. Even while she had been with Juan she hadn't been able to put Raymond out of her mind. She'd never as much as mentioned the word marriage to Raymond, and she had always given him a good time. And she would never even try to . . . . But by now I could endure her no longer. "Elsa," I said, "go to Cyril and ask him as a favor to me if you could possibly stay with his mother. Say you are in need of hospitality. I'm sure he can get his mother to do it. Tell him I'll come to see him tomorrow morning, and the three of us will discuss the situation."

On the doorstep, meaning to be funny, I added: "You are fighting for your future, Elsa!"

She gravely acquiesced as if there were not fifteen or twenty futures in store for her, in the shape of men who would support her. I watched her walking away in the sunshine with her mincing steps. I thought that, before a week had gone by, my father would want her back.

It was then three-thirty. At this moment my father must have been sleeping in Anne's arms, and she too, blooming, weary, filled with the heat of pleasure and happiness, must have given herself to sleep. I began to formulate plans one after another, without pausing to reflect. I walked up and down in my room between the door and the window, looking out from time to time at the calm sea stretched out along the beach. I calculated the risks, estimated possibilities, and gradually I overcame every objection. I felt menacingly clever, and the wave of self-disgust which had swept over me when I first spoke to Elsa now gave place to a feeling of pride in my own capabilities.

I need hardly say that this collapsed when we all went down to swim. As soon as I saw Anne, I was overcome by remorse and did my utmost to atone for my past misbehavior. I carried her bag, I rushed forward with her wrap when she came out of the water. I smothered her with attentions and said the nicest things. This sudden change after my silence of the past few days naturally surprised her. My father was delighted. Anne smiled at me and became very gay. I thought of the words I had used in speaking of her to Elsa. How could I have said them, and how could I have put up with Elsa's nonsense? Tomorrow I would advise Elsa to go away, saying that I had made a mistake. Everything would be as before, and, after all, why should I not try to pass my examination? A college degree was sure to come in useful later on.

"Isn't that so?" I asked Anne. "Isn't it useful to get a college degree?"

She gave me a look and burst out laughing. I followed suit, happy to see her so gay. "You're really incredible!" she exclaimed.

I certainly was incredible, and she would have thought me even more so if she had known what I had been planning. I was dying to tell her all about it so that she should see how incredible I could be. I wanted to tell her: "Can you imagine that I was going to make Elsa pretend to be in love with Cyril? She was to go and stay in his house, and we would have seen them sailing by in his boat, strolling in the woods or along the road. Elsa looks lovely again. Of course she hasn't your beauty. Hers is the flamboyant kind that makes men turn around. My father wouldn't have stood it for long. He could never allow a good-looking woman who had lived with him to take another lover so soon and, so to speak, right before his eyes, and certainly not a man younger than himself. You understand, Anne, he would have wanted her again very quickly even though he loves you, just in order to bolster his morale. He's very vain, or else not very sure of himself, whichever way you like to put it. Elsa, under my direction, would have done all that was necessary. The day would surely come when he would have been unfaithful to you. And you couldn't bear that, could you? You're not one of those women who can share a man. So you would have gone away. And that was exactly what I wanted. It's stupid, I know, but I was angry with you because of Bergson, because of the heat. I somehow imagined . . . I daren't even tell you, it was so ridiculous and unreal. On account of my college exam I might have caused a complete break with you—you, the old friend of my mother, *our* friend . . . And it *is* useful, isn't it, to have a college degree?" Then: "Isn't it?" I said aloud.

"Isn't *what*?" asked Anne. "That a degree is useful?"

"Yes," I replied.

After all, it was better not to tell her anything; perhaps she could not have understood. There were things Anne did not understand at all. I ran into the sea behind my father and wrestled playfully with him. Once more I was able to enjoy frolicking in the water, for now I had a good conscience. Tomorrow I would change my room; I would move up to the attic with my schoolbooks. But Bergson would not be among them; there was no need to overdo it! For two hours every day I would concentrate in solitude on my work. I imagined myself triumphantly passing the examinations in October, and thought of my father's astonished laugh, Anne's approbation, my degree. I would be intelligent, cultured, somewhat aloof, like Anne. Perhaps I had intellectual gifts? Hadn't I been capable of producing a sound, logical plan, despicable perhaps, but logical? And what about Elsa? I had known how to appeal to her vanity and sentimentality, and within a few minutes had managed to persuade her, when her only object in coming back had been to get her suitcase. I felt proud of myself: I had sized up Elsa, found her weak spot, and carefully aimed my words. For the first time in my life I had known the intense pleasure of analyzing another person, manipulating that person toward my own ends. It was a new experience; in the past I had always been too impulsive, and whenever I had come close to understanding someone, it had been pure accident. Now I had caught a sudden glimpse of the marvelous mechanism of human reflexes, and the power that lies in the spoken word. I felt sorry that I had come to it through lies. The day might come when I would love someone passionately, and would have to search warily, gently for the way to reach his heart.

Chapter 3

WALKING down to Cyril's villa the next morning, I felt far less sure of my intellectual prowess. To celebrate my recovery, I had drunk too much at dinner the night before, and had been rather more than gay. I had told my father that I was going to work for a degree, and would associate in future only with highbrows; that I wanted to become famous and a thorough bore. I said he must make use of every scandalous trick known to publicity in order to launch my career. Roaring with laughter, we said the wildest things. Anne laughed, too, but indulgently and not so loudly. When I became too extravagant, she stopped laughing altogether. But our hilarious fun had put my father into such a happy frame of mind that she did not try to stop it. At last they went to bed, after tucking me in. I thanked them from the bottom of my heart, and said what would I ever do without them. My father had no answer, but Anne looked as if she were about to express very decided views on the subject. Just as she leaned over to speak to me, I fell asleep. In the middle of the night I was sick, and my awakening the next morning was the worst I could ever remember. Still feeling very fuzzy and in low spirits, I walked slowly toward the woods, having no eyes for the sea or for the restless seagulls.

Cyril was at his garden gate. He rushed toward me, took me in his arms, and held me tightly, talking incoherently.

"I was so worried! Oh, darling! It's been so long! I had no idea what you were doing, or if that woman was making you suffer. I've never been so miserable. Several times I hung around your cove all afternoon, hoping . . . I had no idea how much I loved you!"

"Neither did I," I said.

To tell the truth, I was both surprised and touched, but I could not express my feelings because I had such a hangover.

"How pale you are!" he said. "From now on I'm going to look after you. I won't let you be ill-treated any more."

I recognized Elsa's exaggerations and asked Cyril what his mother thought of Elsa.

"I introduced her as a friend of yours, an orphan. As a matter of fact, she's very nice; she told me all about *that woman*. How strange it is that with such a delicate, refined face she could be such a low adventuress."

"Elsa is too sensational," I said weakly. "But I am on my way to tell her . . . "

"I, too, have something to tell *you*," interrupted Cyril. "Cécile, I want to marry you."

I had a moment of panic. I absolutely had to do or say

something. If only I did not have this dreadful hangover!

"I love you," said Cyril, speaking into my hair. "I'll give up studying law. An uncle of mine has offered me an interesting job. I'm twenty-six. I'm not a boy any longer. I am serious about this. What do you say?"

I tried desperately to think of a noncommittal, high-sounding phrase. I did not want to marry him. I loved him, yes, but I did not want to marry him. I didn't want to marry anyone; I was tired.

"It's quite impossible," I stammered. "My father ... "

"I'll manage your father," said Cyril.

"Anne wouldn't approve," I said. "She doesn't think I'm grown up. If she says no, my father will say the same. I'm *so* exhausted, Cyril. All this emotion wears me out. Here's Elsa!"

She was wearing a negligee, and looked fresh and radiant. I was spiritless, emaciated. Both Cyril and Elsa were overflowing with health and high spirits, which depressed me even more. She treated me as though I had just escaped from jail, fussed over me. I sat down.

"How is Raymond?" she asked. "Does he know I'm here?"

She had the happy smile of one who has forgiven and is full of hope. How could I tell her that my father had forgotten her existence? How explain to Cyril that I did not want to marry him? I shut my eyes. Cyril went to get some coffee. Elsa talked on and on. She obviously thought me a very subtle person on whom she could

count completely. The coffee was strong and fragrant.
The sun was good and hot. I began to feel a little better.

"I've thought and thought, but without finding a
way out," said Elsa.

"There isn't one," said Cyril. "Your father is infatu-
ated, there's nothing to be done."

"Oh yes, there is!" I said. "You just haven't any imag-
ination."

It flattered me to see how they hung on my words.
They were ten years older than I, and still they had no
ideas! I said with a superior air: "It is a question of psy-
chology."

I went on to explain my plan. They raised the same
objections I had raised to myself the day before and I felt
a particular pleasure in refuting them. I got excited all
over again, in my effort to convince them that my plan
was feasible. When it came to proving why it ought not
to be carried out, my arguments were not so logical.

"I don't like that kind of intrigue," said Cyril reluctantly. "But if it is the only way to make you marry me,
I'll do it."

"That's not entirely up to Anne," I said.

"You know very well that if she stays, you'll have to
marry the man she chooses," said Elsa.

Perhaps that was true. I could see Anne introducing
me on my twentieth birthday to a young man with a
college degree to match my own, assured of a brilliant
future, steady and faithful. In fact, someone like Cyril
himself! I began to laugh.

"Please don't laugh," said Cyril. "Tell me that you'll be jealous when I'm pretending to be in love with Elsa. How can you bear the thought of it for one moment? Do you love me?"

He spoke in a low voice. Elsa had gone off discreetly and left us alone. I looked at Cyril's tense, brown face, his dark eyes. It gave me a strange feeling to think he loved me. I looked at his red lips, so near mine. I did not feel intellectual any longer. He came closer, our lips met and he kissed me passionately. I stayed seated, eyes open, his mouth against mine, hot and hard. A light tremor ran through me. He paused a minute, then his lips opened and our kiss became quickly imperious, skilled, too skilled. I realized that I was more gifted in kissing a young man in the warm sunshine than in taking a degree. I drew away from him, gasping for breath.

"Cécile, we've got to live together, forever! Meanwhile, I'll play the game with Elsa."

I wondered if I was right in my reckoning. Since I was the instigator of the whole thing, I thought, I could always stop it.

"You're so full of ideas," said Cyril with his special smile that lifted one side of his mouth and gave him the appearance of a handsome brigand.

And that is how I set the whole drama in motion, against my better judgment. Sometimes I think I would blame myself less if I had been prompted that day by hatred and violence, and had not allowed myself to drift into it merely through inertia, the sun, and Cyril's kisses.

When I left my fellow conspirators at the end of an hour, I was rather perturbed. However, there were still grounds for reassurance; my plan might well misfire because my father's real passion for Anne would keep him faithful to her. In addition, neither Cyril nor Elsa could do much without my connivance. If my father showed any signs of falling into the trap, I could find some means of putting an end to the whole thing. But still it was amusing to try the plan out, and see whether my psychological judgment proved right or wrong.

Moreover, Cyril was in love with me and had asked me to marry him. This was enough to put me into a pleasant daze. If he could wait two years, to give me time to grow up, I would accept him. I could already imagine myself living with Cyril, sleeping next to him, never leaving him. Every Sunday we would go to lunch with Anne and my father, a happy married couple, and sometimes perhaps we would include Cyril's mother which would add the final touch of domesticity.

I met Anne on the terrace on her way down to the beach to join my father. She received me with that teasing smile with which one greets those who have drunk too much the night before. I asked her what she had been going to say to me just as I fell asleep, but she only laughed and said it might make me cross. Just then my father came out of the water. He was broad and muscular, and I thought he looked wonderful. I went into the water with Anne, who swam slowly with her head well out of the water so she wouldn't wet her hair. Afterward we three lay side by side on our stomachs in the sand, with me in the middle. We were quiet and peaceful.

Just then a boat appeared around the rocks, all sails set. My father was the first to see it.

"So Cyril couldn't hold out any longer!" he said laughing. "Shall we forgive him, Anne? After all, he's a nice boy."

I raised my head, scenting danger.

"But what is he up to?" said my father. "He's not coming in, after all. Ah! He's not alone."

Anne had also turned to look. The boat was passing right in front of our beach, before tacking. I could make out Cyril's features. Silently I prayed that he would disappear, but then I heard my father's exclamation of surprise:

"But it's Elsa! What on earth is she doing there?"

He turned to Anne. "That girl is incredible! She must already have got her claws into that poor boy and made the old lady tolerate her."

But Anne was not listening; she was watching me. I saw her and hid my face in the sand to cover my shame. She put out her hand and touched my neck.

"Look at me. Do you blame me for it?"

I opened my eyes. She bent over me anxiously, almost imploringly. For the first time she was treating me as a sensible person with feelings just on the day when. . . .

I groaned and jerked my head around toward my father to free myself from her hand. He was watching the boat.

"My poor child," Anne was saying in a low voice, "poor little Cécile! I'm afraid it is all my fault. Perhaps I shouldn't have been so hard on you. I never wanted to hurt you. Do you believe me?"

She gently stroked my hair and neck. I kept quite still. I had the same physical sensation as when a receding wave dragged the sand away from under me. Neither anger nor desire had ever worked so strongly in me as my longing at that moment for utter defeat. My one wish was to give up all my plans and put myself entirely into her hands for the rest of my life. I had never before been so overcome with such a sense of utter impotence. I closed my eyes. It seemed to me that my heart stopped beating.

Chapter 4

So far my father had shown no feeling other than surprise. Back at the house, the maid told him that Elsa had been to get her suitcase, but said nothing about her visit with me. Being a peasant woman with a romantic turn of mind, she must have relished the various changes that had taken place in our household since she had been with us, especially in the bedrooms.

My father and Anne, in their effort to make amends, were so kind to me that at first I found it unbearable. However, I soon changed my mind, for even though I had brought it on myself, I did not find it very agreeable to see Cyril and Elsa walking about arm in arm, showing every sign of pleasure in each other's company. I could no longer go sailing with him myself, but I had to watch Elsa passing by, her hair blown by the wind, as mine used to be. It was easy enough for me to look coldly away whenever we met, as we frequently did: in the woods, in the village, and on the road. Anne would glance at me, start a new topic of conversation, and put her hand on my shoulder to comfort me. Have I mentioned before how kind she could be? Whether her kindness emanated from her intelligence, or was merely part of her self-control, I do not know. But she had an unerring instinct for the right, tactful word. If I had really been unhappy over Cyril, I could hardly have found better consolation.

As my father gave no sign of jealousy, I was as yet not unduly worried, so I let things drift. But while it proved to me how fond he was of Anne, I felt rather annoyed that my plan had misfired. One day he and I were on our way to the post office when we passed Elsa. She pretended not to see us, and my father turned after her with a whistle of surprise, as if she had been a stranger.

"I say! Hasn't she become a beauty?"

"Love seems to agree with her," I remarked.

He looked surprised. "You're taking it very well, I must say!"

"What can one expect? Cyril and Elsa are about the same age. I suppose it was inevitable."

"If Anne hadn't come along, it wouldn't have been inevitable at all!" he said angrily. "You don't think I'd let a boy like that snatch a woman from me unless I didn't care?"

"All the same, age counts!" I said solemnly.

He shrugged his shoulders. On the way back I noticed he was preoccupied. Perhaps he was thinking that both Cyril and Elsa were young, and that in marrying a woman of his own age, he would cease to belong to the age group of men who are looked upon as still young. I had a momentary feeling of triumph, but when I saw the tiny wrinkles at the corners of Anne's eyes, and the fine lines around her mouth, I felt ashamed of myself. It was only too easy to follow my impulses and repent afterward.

A week went by. Cyril and Elsa, who had no idea how matters were progressing, must have been expecting me every day. I was afraid to go and see them for fear I would be tempted to try something else. Every afternoon I went up to my room, ostensibly to study, but in fact I did nothing. I found a book on Yoga and spent my time practicing various exercises. I took care to smother my laughter in case Anne should hear. I told her I was working hard. I pretended that my disappointment in love had made me keen to get my degree as a consolation. I hoped this would raise me in her estimation, and I even went so far as to quote Kant at table, to my father's dismay.

One afternoon I had wrapped myself in bath towels to look like a Hindu, and was sitting cross-legged staring at myself in the mirror, hoping to achieve a Yoga-like trance, when there was a knock at the door. I thought it was the maid and told her to come in.

It was Anne. For a moment she remained transfixed in the doorway, then she smiled.

"What are you playing at?"

"Yoga," I replied, "But it's not a game at all. It's a Hindu philosophy."

She went to the table and took up my book. I began to

be worried. It was open at page one hundred and the preceding pages were covered with remarks in my handwriting, such as "too hard" or "exhausting."

"You are certainly conscientious," she said. "And what about that essay you're writing on Pascal? I don't see it anywhere."

At lunch I had been talking about Pascal, implying that I was working on a certain passage, but, needless to say, I had not written a word. Anne waited for me to say something, but as I did not reply, she understood.

"It is your own business if you play the fool up here instead of working, but it's quite another matter when you lie to your father and me. I must admit it was hard to believe in this sudden intellectual activity."

She went out of the room, leaving me petrified in my bath towels. I could not understand why she had used the word "lie." I had spoken of Pascal because it amused me, and had mentioned my essay to make her happy, and now she blamed me for it. I had grown used to her new, tolerant attitude toward me, and her contempt made me feel humiliated and furious. I threw off my disguise, pulled on some slacks and an old shirt and rushed out of the house.

The heat was terrific, but I began to run, impelled by my anger, which was all the more violent because it was mixed with shame. I ran all the way to Cyril's villa, stopping only when I reached his door to regain my breath. In the afternoon heat, the house seemed unnaturally large and quiet, full of secrets. I crept silently up to

Cyril's room; he had showed it to me the day we called on his mother. I opened the door. Cyril was lying across the bed, fast asleep with his head on his arm. I stood looking at him. For the first time he seemed vulnerable and rather touching. I called to him in a low voice. He opened his eyes and sat up at once.

"You, Cécile! What's the matter?"

I signed to him not to talk so loudly. Suppose his mother were to come and find me in his room? She might think . . . wouldn't anyone think . . . ? Suddenly I felt panic-stricken and moved toward the door.

"But don't go away!" he cried. "Come here, Cécile!"

He caught me by the wrist and, laughing, kept me from moving. I turned around to him and saw him suddenly grow pale, as I must have done myself. He let go my wrist, but only to take me in his arms and draw me over to the bed. It has to happen sometime, I was thinking in my confusion, it has to happen. . . .

For this was the round of love: fear which leads on desire, tenderness and fury, and that brutal anguish which triumphantly follows pleasure. I was lucky enough—thanks to Cyril's gentleness—to discover it all that day.

I stayed with him for about an hour. I was happy, but bewildered. I was used to hearing the word love bandied about, and I had often talked about it stupidly myself, as one does when one is young and ignorant. But now I felt I could never talk of love again in that brutal, detached manner.

Cyril, lying beside me, was going on about marrying me and how we would be together always. My silence made him uneasy. I sat up, looked tenderly at him, and murmured: "My lover!" I kissed the vein on his neck, murmuring, "Darling, darling Cyril!"

I was not so sure it was love I felt for him at that moment. I have always been fickle, and I have no wish to delude myself on this point. But just then I loved him more than I loved myself; I would have sacrificed my life for him. When I left him, he asked me if I was angry with him. I just laughed! How could I possibly be angry with him when he had given me such pleasure?

I walked slowly back through the pine woods. I had asked Cyril not to come with me; it would have been too risky. Besides, I was afraid something might show in my face or manner. Anne was lying on a deck chair in front of the house, reading. I had made up a story to explain where I had been. I did not need to use it. She never asked questions. Then I remembered we had quarreled, and I sat down near her in dead silence. I remained motionless, aware of my own breathing and the trembling of my fingers, and thinking of Cyril.

I got a cigarette from the table and struck a match. It went out. With shaking hands I struck another match, and although there was no wind, it, too, went out. In exasperation I took a third, and for some reason this match assumed a vital importance, perhaps because Anne was watching me intently. Suddenly everything around me seemed to melt away and there was nothing

left but the match between my fingers, the box, and
Anne's eyes boring into me. My heart was beating violently. I tightened my fingers around the match and
struck it, but as I bent forward, my cigarette put it out.
The matchbox dropped to the ground and I could feel
Anne's hard, searching gaze upon me. The tension was
unbearable. Then her hands were under my chin, and
as she raised my face, I shut my eyes tightly for fear she
should read their expression and see the tears welling
up, tears of fatigue, of pleasure, of shame. She stroked
my cheek, and then let me go, as if she had decided to
leave things be. Then she lit a cigarette, put it into my
mouth and returned to her book.

Perhaps the incident was symbolic. Sometimes when
I am groping for a match, I find myself thinking of that
strange moment when my hands no longer seemed to
belong to me, and again I recall the intensity of Anne's
look, and the emptiness around me—the vast emptiness.

Chapter 5

THE incident I have just described was not without its aftermath. Like some self-controlled, self-assured persons, Anne did not like to make compromises. When, on the terrace, she had let me go, she was acting against her principles. She had, of course, guessed something, and it would have been easy enough for her to make me talk. But finally she had yielded to pity or indifference. It was just as hard for her to make allowances for my shortcomings as to try to remove them. In both cases she was prompted merely by a sense of duty. In marrying my father she felt she must also take charge of me. I would have found it easier to accept her constant disapproval if she had sometimes shown exasperation, or any other feeling which went more than skin-deep. One gets used to other people's faults if one does not feel it a duty to correct them. Within a few months she would have ceased to trouble about me and her indifference might then have been tempered by affection. This attitude would have suited me down to the ground. But it could never happen with her, because her sense of responsibility was too strong, especially since I was still young enough to be influenced. I was malleable, though obstinate.

Therefore she had a feeling of frustration concerning me. She was annoyed with herself and let me see it. A few days later we were at dinner when the controversial subject of my vacation tasks cropped up. I was a bit too off-hand, and even my father showed annoyance. But in the end it was Anne who locked me up in my room, although she had not even raised her voice during the argument. I had no idea what she had done until I tried to leave the room to get a glass of water. I had never been locked up, and at first I was in a panic. I rushed over to the window, but there was no escape that way. Then I threw myself against the door so violently that I bruised my shoulder. With my teeth clenched I tried to force the lock with a pair of tweezers. I did not want to call to anyone to open it. After that I stood still in the middle of the room, tried to collect my thoughts, and gradually I became quite calm. This was my first contact with cruelty. I felt it grow in me, as my thoughts gave it substance. I lay stretched out, on my bed, and began to plan my revenge. My ferocity was entirely out of proportion to the cause. In fact several times I went to open the door, and was surprised to find that I could not get out.

At six o'clock my father came to release me. I got up when he came in, and smiled at him. He looked at me in silence.

"Have you anything to say to me as yet?" he asked.

"What about?" I said. "You know we both have a horror of explanations that lead nowhere."

He seemed relieved. "But do try to be nicer to Anne, more patient."

His choice of words surprised me: *me* be patient with Anne? Instead of the other way round. I realized that he thought of Anne as a woman he was imposing on his daughter, instead of the contrary. There was evidently still room for hope.

"I was horrid," I said. "I'll apologize to her."

"You're not unhappy, are you?"

"Of course not!" I replied. "And, anyhow, if she and I quarrel too often, I shall just marry a little earlier, that's all!" I knew my words would strike home.

"You mustn't look at it in that way. You're not Snow White! You wouldn't go away and leave me so soon? We've only had two years together."

The thought was as unbearable for me as for him. I could see myself crying on his shoulder, bewailing our lost happiness. But I would not involve him in my conspiracy.

"You know I always exaggerate. With a few concessions on both sides, Anne and I will get on all right."

"Yes," he said. "Of course!"

He must have thought, as I did at that moment, that the concessions would probably not be mutual, but would be on my side only.

"You see," I told him. "I realize very well that Anne

is always right. Her way of living is really far more
satisfactory than ours, has greater depth."

He started to protest, but I went on: "In a month or
two I shall have completely assimilated Anne's ideas,
and there won't be any more stupid arguments between
us. It just needs patience."

He was obviously taken aback. He was not only losing a boon companion, but a slice of his past as well.

"Now don't exaggerate again!" he said in a weak
voice. "I know that the kind of life you have led with
me was perhaps not suitable for your age, or mine either,
for that matter, but it was neither dull nor gloomy. After
all, we've never been bored or depressed during the
last two years, have we? There's no need to be so dras-
tic, just because Anne's conception of life is a little
different."

"On the contrary," I said firmly. "We'll have to go
even further than I mentioned, give up our old way of
life altogether!"

"Oh, I suppose so," said my poor father as we went
downstairs together.

I made my apologies to Anne without the slightest
embarrassment. She told me that I needn't have bothered; the heat must have been the cause of our dispute.
I felt gay and carefree.

I met Cyril in the pine woods, as we had planned. I
told him what to do next. He listened to me with a mixture of fear and admiration. Then he took me in his arms,
but I could not stay as it was getting late. I was sur-

prised to find that I did not want to leave him. If he had
been searching for the means of attaching me to him,
he had certainly found it. My body responded to his
and bloomed beside him. I kissed him passionately,
I even wanted to bruise him, so that he would not be
able to forget me for a single moment all the evening,
and would dream of me all night long. I could not bear
the thought of the night without him, close to me, without his sudden fury and his long caresses.

Chapter 6

THE next morning I took my father for a walk along the road. We talked gaily of frivolous matters. I suggested going back to the villa by way of the pine woods. It was exactly half-past ten; just the right time. My father was walking in front of me on the narrow path, pushing aside the brambles so that I should not scratch my legs. When he stopped dead in his tracks I knew he had seen them. I went up to him. There they were, Cyril and Elsa, lying on the pine needles, apparently asleep. Although they were acting entirely on my instructions, and I knew very well that they were not in love, nevertheless they were both young and beautiful, and I could not help feeling a pang of jealousy. I saw that my father was white as a sheet. I took him by the arm.

"Don't let's disturb them. Come on!"

He glanced once more at Elsa, who lay there in all her youthful beauty, all golden, with her red hair and with a half smile on her lips. She seemed indeed a young nymph trapped at last by love. Then he turned on his heel and walked on at a brisk pace. I could hear him muttering: "The bitch! The bitch!"

"Why do you say that? She's free, isn't she?"

"That's not the point! Did you find it very pleasant to see her in Cyril's arms?"

"I don't love him any more," I said.

"Neither do I love Elsa," he answered furiously. "But it hurts just the same. After all, I have . . . ah . . . lived with her. That makes it worse."

Did I know that made it worse? Yes, indeed! He must have felt like dashing up to tear them apart and seize his property—or what had once been his property.

"Suppose Anne were to hear you say such a thing!" I said.

"What do you mean? Well, of course she wouldn't understand. She'd be shocked, that's normal enough! But what about you? Don't you understand me any more? Are you shocked, too?"

How easy it was for me to steer his thoughts in the direction I wanted! It was rather frightening to know him so well.

"Of course I'm not shocked," I said. "But you must see things as they are. Elsa has a short memory, she finds Cyril attractive, and that's the end of it as far as you're concerned. After all, look how you behaved to her. It was unforgivable!"

"If I wanted her . . . " my father began and then stopped short.

"You'd have no luck," I said positively, as if it were the most natural thing in the world for me to discuss his chances of getting Elsa back.

"Anyhow it is out of the question," he said in a more resigned voice.

"Of course it is!" I answered with a shrug of my shoulders which was meant to convey that he, poor chap, was out of the running now. He said not another word until we reached the house. Then he took Anne into his arms and held her close to him. She was surprised, but submitted happily to his embrace. I went out of the room, trembling with shame.

At two o'clock, I heard a soft whistle, and went down to join Cyril on the beach. We got into his boat and sailed out to sea. There was nothing in sight; no one else was out in that heat. When we were some way from the shore, he pulled down the sail. So far we had hardly exchanged a word.

"This morning," he began.

"Don't talk," I said. "Oh, please don't talk."

He gently pushed me down in the boat. We were awash, sweaty, awkward and urgent. I could feel the boat swaying as we made love. I watched the sun above me. Suddenly there was the tender, imperious whisper of Cyril. The sun exploded and fell on me. Where was I? At the bottom of the sea, at the bottom of time, at the bottom of pleasure. I called Cyril in a loud voice. He did not answer. He did not have to answer.

Afterward there was the tang of salt water. We lay in the sun, laughed and were happy. We had the sun and the sea, laughter and love: I wonder if either he or I shall ever again recover the particular brilliance of those days. And for me they were heightened by an undercurrent of anxiety and remorse.

I found, beyond the very real physical pleasure of love, a kind of intellectual pleasure in thinking about it. The words "to make," material and positive, united with the poetical abstraction of the word "love," enchanted me. I had said them before without the least embarrassment or without noticing their special savor. Now I found myself prudish. I lowered my gaze when my father turned his eyes to Anne as she laughed her low laugh, indecently intimate, which made us pale, my father and me, and look out of the window. Had we told Anne that her laugh revealed her so, she would not have believed us. She did not act like a mistress with my father, but like a friend, a tender friend. But in the night ... I turned from such thoughts, I hated such disturbing ideas.

The time passed quickly. I almost forgot Anne, my father, and Elsa. Through love I had entered another world. I felt dreamy, yet wide awake, peaceful and contented. Cyril asked me if I were not afraid of having a child. I told him that I was entirely in his hands, and he seemed satisfied that it should be so. Perhaps I had given myself to him because I knew that if I had a child, he would be prepared to take the blame. He was ready to take on what I could never face: responsibility. Besides, I could not imagine myself pregnant, with my slight, hard body. . . . For once I was thankful for my adolescent figure.

But Elsa was growing impatient. She plied me with questions. I was always afraid of being seen with her or Cyril. She lay in wait for my father at every likely spot, and tried to convince herself that he had difficulty in keeping away from her. I was surprised that this woman of pleasure, who had always associated love with money, should get such romantic ideas, be excited by a look or a gesture, when such things had usually been merely routine for her. The role she was playing evidently seemed to her the height of psychological subtlety.

Though my father was gradually becoming obsessed with the thought of Elsa, Anne did not seem to notice it. He was more affectionate and demonstrative than ever with her, which frightened me, because I attributed it to his subconscious guilt. In three weeks we should be back in Paris, and the main thing was that nothing should happen before then. Elsa would be out of our way, and my father and Anne would get married if by then they had not changed their minds. In Paris I would have Cyril, and just as Anne had been unable to keep us apart here, so she would find it impossible to stop me from seeing him once we were home. In Paris, Cyril had a room away from his mother. I could already imagine the window open to the pink and blue sky, the wonderful sky of Paris, with the pigeons cooing on the window sill, and with Cyril beside me on the narrow bed. . . .

Chapter 7

A FEW days later my father received a message from one of our friends asking us to meet him at a café in Saint Raphael for a drink. He was pleased at the thought of escaping for a while from this unusual seclusion in which we had chosen to live. He could hardly wait to tell us the news. I mentioned to Elsa and Cyril that we would be at the Bar du Soleil at seven o'clock and if they liked to come, they would see us there. Then I learned that Elsa happened to know the friend we were meeting which made her all the more keen to go. So I realized that there might be complications, and tried in vain to put her off.

"Charles Webb simply adores me," she said, with childlike simplicity. "If he sees me, his response is sure to make Raymond want to come back to me."

Cyril did not care whether he went to Saint Raphael or not. I saw by the way he looked at me that he wanted only to be near me, and I felt proud.

At six o'clock we drove off in Anne's car. It was a huge American convertible, which she kept more for publicity than to suit her own taste, but it suited mine down to the ground, with all its shiny gadgets. Another advantage was that we could all three sit in front, and I never felt so happy as when I was in a car with the two of them, elbow to elbow, sharing the same pleasures, and perhaps even the same death. Anne was at the wheel, as if symbolizing her future place in the family. This was the first time I had been in her car since the evening we went to Cannes.

We met Charles Webb and his wife at the Bar du Soleil. He was engaged in theatrical publicity; his wife spent all his earnings on entertaining young men. Money was an obsession with him. He thought of nothing else in his unceasing effort to make ends meet; hence his restless impatience. He had been Elsa's lover for a long time, and she had suited him quite well, because, though very pretty, she was not particularly grasping.

His wife was a malicious woman. Anne had never met her, and I noticed that Anne's lovely face quickly assumed the superior, mocking expression that was habitual with her in society. As usual Charles Webb talked all the time, now and then giving Anne an inquisitive look. He evidently wondered how Anne came to be with that notorious lady-killer, Raymond, and his daughter. I was glad to think he would soon find out. Just then my father leaned forward and said abruptly:

"I have news for you, old chap. Anne and I are getting married on the fifth of October."

Webb looked from one to the other in amazement. His wife, who had rather a weakness for my father, seemed disconcerted.

After a pause, Webb shouted: "Congratulations! What a splendid idea! My dear lady, you don't know what you're taking on! You are wonderful! Here, waiter! We must celebrate!"

Anne smiled quietly and calmly. Then I saw Webb's face light up; I had no need to turn around.

"Elsa! Good heavens! It's Elsa Mackenbourg! She hasn't noticed me yet. I say, Raymond, do you see how lovely that girl has grown?"

"Hasn't she?" said my father in a proprietary tone, but then he remembered, and his face fell.

Anne could hardly help noticing that inflection in his voice. She turned to me with a quick movement, but before she could speak I leaned toward her and said in a confidential whisper, loud enough for my father to hear:

"Anne, you're causing quite a sensation. There's a man over there who can't take his eyes off you."

My father twisted around to look at the man in question.

"I won't tolerate that sort of thing!" he said, taking Anne's hand.

"Aren't they sweet?" exclaimed Mrs. Webb, ironically. "Charles, we really shouldn't have disturbed them. It would have been better to have invited little Cécile all by herself."

"Little Cécile wouldn't have come," I said unhesitatingly.

"Why not? Are you in love with one of the fishermen?"

Mrs. Webb had once seen me in conversation with a bus conductor, and ever since had treated me as though I had lost caste.

"Why yes, of course!" I said with an effort to appear gay.

"And do you go out fishing a lot with him?"

She thought she was being witty, which made it worse. I was beginning to get angry.

"I don't specialize in mackerel," I said. "But I do go fishing."

There was a dead silence. They evidently understood my pun. Anne's voice interposed quietly:

"Raymond, would you mind asking the waiter to bring me a straw to drink my orange juice?"

Charles Webb began to talk feverishly about having another round of drinks. I could see from the way my father was staring into his glass that he was longing to laugh. Anne gave me a look of entreaty. Nevertheless we all decided to dine together, just to show there were no hard feelings.

At dinner I drank too much. I wanted to forget Anne's anxious expression when she looked at my father, and the hint of gratitude in her eyes whenever they rested on me. Every time Mrs. Webb made a dig at me I answered it with an ingratiating smile. This seemed to upset her, and she soon became openly aggressive. Anne signed to me to keep quiet. She had a horror of scenes in public, and Mrs. Webb was on the verge of creating one. For my part, I was used to them. Among our associates, they were frequent, so I was not disturbed by the prospect.

After dinner we went to another bar. Soon Elsa and Cyril turned up. Elsa was talking very loud as she entered the room followed by poor Cyril. I thought she was behaving badly, but she was pretty enough to carry it off.

"Who's that puppy she's with?" asked Charles Webb. "He's rather young, isn't he?"

"It's love that keeps him young!" simpered his wife.

"Don't you believe it!" said my father. "She's not in love with him. He's just a passing fancy."

I had my eyes on Anne. She was watching Elsa in the calm, detached way she looked at very young women, or at the mannequins who exhibited her creations. For a moment I admired her tremendously for showing no trace of jealousy or spite. But how could she be jealous, I wondered, when she herself was a hundred times more beautiful and intelligent than Elsa? As I was very drunk, I told her so. She looked at me curiously.

"Do you really think I am more beautiful than Elsa?"

"Of course!"

"That is always pleasant to hear. But you are drinking too much again. Give me your drink. I hope it doesn't upset you to see Cyril here. Anyway, he seems bored to death."

"He's my lover," I said with gay abandon.

"You *are* quite drunk! Thank goodness, it's time to go home."

It was a relief to part from the Webbs. I found it difficult to say good-by politely. My father drove the car, and my head lolled onto Anne's shoulder.

I was thinking how much I preferred her to the people we usually saw, how infinitely superior she was in every way. My father said very little; perhaps he was thinking of Elsa.

"Is she sleeping?" he asked Anne.

"As peaceful as a baby. She didn't behave badly on the whole, did she? Of course she should not have made that remark about mackerel."

My father laughed. They were silent for a while, then I heard his voice again:

"Anne, I love you, only you. Do you believe me?"

"Don't tell me so often. It frightens me."

"Give me your hand."

I almost sat up to protest: "For heaven's sake, not on the Corniche!" But I was too drunk, and still half asleep. Besides, there was Anne's perfume, the sea breeze in my hair, the little scratch on my shoulder was a reminder of Cyril's love making, all these reasons to be happy and keep quiet. I thought of Elsa and Cyril setting off on the motorcycle which had been a birthday present from his mother. I felt so sorry for them that I almost cried. Anne's car was made for sleeping. It rode so gently, not noisy like a motorcycle. I thought of Mrs. Webb lying

awake at night. No doubt at her age I would also have
to pay someone to love me, because love is the most
wonderful thing in the world. Love was worth whatever it cost. The important thing was not to become
embittered and jealous, as she was of Elsa and Anne. I
began to laugh softly to myself. Anne shifted her shoulder to make a comfortable hollow for me.

"Go to sleep," she ordered.

I went to sleep.

Chapter 8

THE next morning I woke up feeling perfectly well except for a slight ache in my neck. My bed was flooded with sunshine as it was every morning. I threw back the sheets and exposed my bare back to the sun. It was warm and comforting, and seemed to penetrate my very bones. I decided to spend the morning like that, without moving.

In my mind I went over the events of the evening before. I remembered telling Anne that Cyril was my lover. It amused me to think that if one told the truth when drunk, nobody believed it. I thought about Mrs. Webb. I was used to that sort of woman; in circles like hers and at her age they often become unpleasant through lack of enough opportunities to indulge themselves. Anne's calm dignity had shown Mrs. Webb up as even more idiotic and boring than usual. It was only to be expected. I could not imagine anyone among my father's old friends who could for a moment bear comparison with Anne. In order to be able to face an evening with people like that, one had either to be rather drunk and enjoy quarreling with them, or else be on intimate terms with one or other of the group. For my

father it was easy: Charles Webb and he were both
libertines. "Guess who is dining and sleeping with me
tonight? The little Mars girl, in Saurel's latest film. I
was going into Dupuis' house and . . ." then my father
would laugh and tap him on the shoulder.

"Lucky man! She's almost as pretty as Elsa."

Undergraduate talk, but I liked their liveliness. Then
there were interminable evenings on café terraces, and
Lombard's tales of woe. "She was the only one I ever
really loved, Raymond! Do you remember that spring,
before she left me? "It is stupid for a man to devote his
whole life to one woman." All this touched on the indecent, this embarrassing but hot-blooded talk of two
men who told "all" over a drink.

Anne's friends probably never talked about themselves. Perhaps they did not indulge in such adventures.
Or if they spoke of them at all, it would be with an
apologetic laugh. Already I almost shared Anne's condescending attitude toward our friends; it was catch-
ing. On the other hand, by the age of thirty, I could
imagine myself being more like them than like Anne,
and then her silence, her detachment and her reserve
might suffocate me. In fifteen years, a little blasé, I
would lean seductively to an equally world-weary man
and say:

"My first lover was called Cyril. I was almost eigh-
teen, it was hot by the sea. . . . "

I imagined the man's face. He would have little
wrinkles like my father.

There was a knock at the door. I quickly put on my pajama top and called, "Come in!" Anne stood there, carefully holding a cup.

"I thought you might like some coffee. How do you feel this morning?"

"Very well," I answered. "I'm afraid I was a bit tipsy last night."

"As you are each time you go out!" She began to laugh. "But I must say, you were amusing. It was such a tedious evening."

I had forgotten the sun, and even my coffee. When I was talking to Anne, I was completely absorbed. I did not think of myself, and yet she was the only one who made me question my motives. Through her I lived more intensely.

"Cécile, do you really find people like the Webbs and the Dupuis entertaining?"

"Well, they usually behave abominably, but they *are* funny."

She was watching a fly on the floor. Anne's eyelids were long and heavy; it was easy for her to look condescending.

"Don't you ever realize how monotonous and dull their conversation is? Don't those endless stories about girls, business contracts and drinking parties bore you?"

"I'm afraid," I answered, "that after ten years of convent life their lack of morals fascinates me."

I did not dare to add that I also liked it.

"For two years?" she said. "It's not a question of

reason, however, or of morals. It is a question of one's sensibility, a sixth sense."

I supposed I didn't have it. I saw clearly that I was lacking in this respect.

"Anne," I asked abruptly, "do you think I am intelligent?"

She began to laugh, surprised at the directness of my question.

"Of course you are! Why do you ask?"

"If I were an idiot, you'd say just the same thing," I sighed. "I so often find your superiority overpowering."

"It's just a question of age," she answered. "It would be a sad thing if I didn't have a little more self-assurance than you or *you* would dominate *me*!"

She laughed, but I was annoyed.

"That wouldn't necessarily be a bad thing."

"It would be a catastrophe," she said quietly.

She suddenly stopped her bantering tone and looked me straight in the face. I at once felt ill at ease, and began to fidget. Even today I cannot get used to people who stare at me, while they are talking, or come very close to make sure that I am listening. My only thought is to escape. I go on saying "Yes" while gradually edging away. Their insistence and pertinacity enrage me. What right have they to try to corner me? Fortunately Anne did not resort to all these tactics, but she did keep her eyes fixed on me, so that I could no longer talk in the lighthearted vein I usually affected.

"Do you realize how men like Webb end up?" she said.

I thought, "And men like my father."

"In the river," I answered flippantly.

"A time comes when they are no longer attractive or in good form. They can't drink any more, and they still hanker after women. Only then they have to pay heavily and lower their standards, to escape from their loneliness. Then they are really laughingstocks. They grow sentimental and querulous. I have seen many who have gone that way."

"Poor Webb!" I said.

I was impressed. So that was the fate in store for my father? Or at least the fate from which Anne was saving him.

"You never thought of that, did you?" said Anne, with a little smile of commiseration. "You don't think much about the future, do you? But that is the privilege of youth."

"Please don't throw my youth at me like that! I use it neither as an excuse, nor as a privilege. I just don't attach any importance to it."

"To what *do* you attach importance? To your peace of mind? Your freedom?"

I dreaded conversations of this sort, especially with Anne.

"To nothing at all," I said. "You know very well I hardly ever think."

"You and your father irritate me at times. You haven't given it a thought. You're not good for anything. You don't know. Are you really content to be like that?"

"I'm not content with myself. I don't like myself, and I don't try to. At moments you force me to complicate my life, and I hold it against you."

She began to hum to herself, with a thoughtful expression. I recognized the tune, but did not know what it was.

"What's the name of that song, Anne? It gets on my nerves."

"I don't know," she smiled again, looking rather discouraged. "Stay in bed and rest. I'll continue my research on the family intellect somewhere else."

I thought it was easy enough for my father to get out of it. I could just imagine his saying, "I'm not thinking of anything except that I love you, Anne." In spite of her intelligence, Anne would accept this as a valid excuse. I indulged myself in a good stretch and pushed my head deep into my pillow. Anne was dramatizing the situation, I thought. In twenty-five years my father would be an amiable man of sixty-five with white hair, rather addicted to whisky and high-colored reminiscences. We would go out together; it would be my turn to tell him *my* adventures, and his to advise me. I realized that in my mind I was excluding Anne from our future; I did not see how she could fit in.

In the turmoil of our disorderly Paris flat, sometimes

forlorn, at others full of flowers, the stage of many and varied scenes, often cluttered up with luggage, I somehow could not envisage the introduction of order, the peace and quiet, the feeling of harmony that Anne brought with her everywhere, as if they were the most precious of gifts. I dreaded being bored to death. But I was less apprehensive of her influence since my love affair with Cyril, which had liberated me from many of my anxieties. Still, I feared boredom and tranquillity more than anything else. In order to achieve inner peace, my father and I had to have excitement. And this Anne was not prepared to admit.

Chapter 9

I HAVE spoken a great deal about Anne and myself, and very little of my father. Yet he has played the most important part in this story, and my feelings for him have been deeper and more stable than for anyone else. I know him too well, and feel too close to him to talk easily of him, and it is he above all others whom I wish to justify and present in a good light. He was neither vain nor selfish, but just incurably frivolous. I could not call him irresponsible or incapable of deep feelings. His love for me is not to be taken lightly, or regarded merely as a parental habit. He could suffer more through me than through anyone else, and, for my part, I was nearer to despair the day he turned away as if abandoning me, than I had ever been in my life. I was always more important to him than his love affairs. On many evenings, by taking me home from parties, he must have often missed what his friend Webb would have called "a fine chance." On the other hand, I cannot deny that he was inconstant and would always take the easiest way. He never meditated. He tried to give everything a physiological explanation,

which he called being rational. "You don't like yourself
as you are? Just sleep a little more and drink a little less!"
It was the same when at times he had a violent desire for
a particular woman. He never thought of repressing it,
or trying to elevate it into a deeper sentiment. He was a
materialist, if kind and understanding, with a touch of
delicacy. His desire for Elsa disturbed him, though not
in the way one might expect. He did not say to himself:
"I want to be unfaithful to Anne, therefore I must love
her less," but: "This need for Elsa is a nuisance. I must
get over it quickly or it might cause complications with
Anne." Moreover he loved and admired Anne. She was
a change from the stupid, frivolous women he had
known in recent years. She satisfied his vanity, his sen-
suality and his sensibility all at once, for she understood
him. She offered her intelligence and experience to sup-
plement his. Yet I do not believe he realized how deeply
she cared for him. He thought of her as the ideal mistress,
the ideal mother for me, however I do not think he
visualized her as the ideal wife for himself—with all the
obligations this would entail. I am sure that in Cyril's
and in Anne's eyes he was, like me, abnormal, so to
speak. Still the fact that he had no high regard for his
way of living did not prevent him from making it exciting or putting all his vitality into it.

I was not really concerned about him when I formed
the project of shutting Anne out of our lives; I knew he
would console himself with someone else, as he always
had. A clean break with Anne would in the long run

be less painful than living a well-regulated life as her husband. What really would destroy him, as it would me, was being subjected to fixed habits. We were of the same race. Sometimes I thought we belonged to a pure and beautiful race of nomads, and at others to a poor, withered breed of sensualists.

At that moment he was suffering, or at least he was feeling exasperated. Elsa had become the symbol of youth and his recent gay life, above all of his own youth. I knew he was dying to say to Anne:

"Dearest, let me go for just one day. I must prove to myself, with Elsa's help, that I'm not an old fogey."

Now that was impossible, not because Anne was jealous, or too virtuous to discuss such matters, but because she had made up her mind to live with him on her own terms. She was determined to put an end to the era of frivolity and debauchery and to stop his schoolboy behavior. She was entrusting her life to him and in future he must behave well and not be a slave to his caprices. One could not blame Anne; hers was a perfectly normal and sane point of view. Yet it did not keep my father from wanting Elsa, from desiring her more and more as time passed and she was still unobtainable.

At that moment I have no doubt that I could have arranged everything. I had only to tell Elsa to meet him and let him have a quick fling. I could easily have persuaded Anne to go with me to Nice for a whole afternoon on some pretext. On our return we would have found my father relaxed, and filled with a new appre-

ciation of legalized affection, or, rather, affection short-
ly to become legalized. But Anne could not have borne
the idea of having been a mistress like the others. How
difficult she made life for us through her dignity and
self-respect.

But I said nothing to Elsa, neither did I ask Anne to
go to Nice with me. I wanted my father's desire to fester
in him, so that in the end he would give himself away.
I could not bear the contempt with which Anne treated
our past life, her disdain for what had been our happiness. I had no wish to humiliate her, but only to force
her to accept our way of life. For this it was necessary
that she should discover my father's infidelity, should
see it objectively as a physical indulgence, not as an
attack on her personal dignity. If at all costs she wanted
to be right, she must allow us to be wrong.

I even pretended not to notice my father's plight. On
no account would I become his intermediary by speaking to Elsa for him, or getting Anne out of the way. I
had to pretend to look upon Anne and his love for her
as sacred, and I must admit it was not difficult for me.
The idea that he could be unfaithful and defy her filled
me with terror and a vague awe.

Meanwhile we had many happy days. I made use of
every occasion to further my father's interest in Elsa.
The sight of Anne's face no longer filled me with remorse. I sometimes imagined that she would accept
everything, and that we would be able to live a life that
suited us all three equally well. I saw Cyril often. We

made love in secret and I was under the spell of the scent of pines, the sound of the sea, and the contact of his body. . . .

Cyril began to torment himself. He hated the role I had forced upon him, and continued in it only because I made him believe it was necessary for our love. All this involved a great deal of deceit, and much had to be concealed. But it did not cost me much effort to tell a few lies, and after all, I alone was in control, was the sole judge of my actions.

I will pass quickly over this period, for I am afraid that if I look at it closely, I shall revive memories that are too painful. Even now I feel overwhelmed as I think of Anne's happy laugh, of her kindness to me. My conscience troubles me so much at these moments that I am obliged to resort to some expedient like lighting a cigarette, putting on a record, or telephoning to a friend. Then gradually I begin to think of something else. But I do not like having to take refuge in forgetfulness and frivolity instead of facing my memories and fighting them.

Chapter 10

FATE sometimes assumes strange forms. And that summer it appeared in the guise of Elsa, a mediocre person, although attractive. She had an extraordinary laugh, sudden and infectious, the kind that only rather stupid people possess.

I had soon noticed the effect of this laugh on my father. I told her to make the utmost use of it whenever we "surprised" her with Cyril. My orders were: "When you hear me coming with my father, say nothing, just laugh." And at the sound of that laugh a look of fury would come into my father's face. My role of stage manager continued to be exciting. I never missed my mark, for when we saw Cyril and Elsa openly showing signs of their imaginary relationship, my father and I both grew pale with the intensity of our feelings. The sight of Cyril bending over Elsa made my heart ache. I would have given anything in the world to stop them, forgetting for the moment that it was I who had planned it.

Apart from these incidents, our daily life was filled with Anne's confidence, gentleness, and (I hate to use the word) her happiness. She was nearer to happiness than I had ever seen her since she had been with us, egotists that we were. She was far removed from our violent desires and my base little schemes. I counted on her aloofness and instinctive pride to keep her from using any special effort to hold my father to her, counted on her relying only on her beauty, her intelligence, her own loving self. I began to feel sorry for her, and pity is an agreeable sentiment, uplifting like military music.

One fine morning the maid, visibly worked up, handed me a note from Elsa:

"All goes well. Come!"

I had a feeling of imminent catastrophe. I hate theatrical denouements. I met Elsa on the beach; she was looking triumphant.

"I have just been talking to your father, just an hour ago."

"What did he say?"

"He told me he was very sorry for what had happened, that he had behaved like a cad. That's the truth, isn't it?"

I thought it best to agree.

"Then he paid me compliments in the way only he can, you know, quietly, in a low voice, as if at the same time he was suffering."

I interrupted her.

"What was he leading up to?"

"Well, nothing. . . . Oh yes, he asked me to have tea

with him in the village to show I had no ill-feeling, and that I was forgiving. Shall I go?"

My father's views on the need for forgiving natures in red-headed girls were a treat to hear. I came near saying that it didn't matter to me. Then I realized that she credited me with this success. Nevertheless, it irritated me. I felt trapped.

"I don't know, Elsa. That depends on you. You always ask me what you should do. One might almost believe that it was I who induced you . . . "

"But it was you," she said. "It's entirely through you that . . . "

The admiration in her voice suddenly frightened me.

"Go if you want to, but for heaven's sake, don't talk any more about it!"

"But, Cécile, isn't the whole idea to free him from that woman's clutches?"

I fled. Let my father do as he wished, and Anne must deal with it as best she could. Anyhow, I was on my way to meet Cyril. It seemed to me that love was the only remedy for the haunting anxiety I felt.

Cyril took me in his arms. Without a word he led me away. With him everything became easy, charged as it was with ardor and with pleasure. Later, stretched out beside his sunburned body, bathed in perspiration, I was drained of feeling, lost like a shipwrecked soul, and I told him that I hated myself. I smiled as I said it because, although I meant it, there was no pain, only an enjoyable resignation. He did not take me seriously.

"Never mind. I love you so much that I shall make you feel about yourself as I do."

All through our midday meal, I thought of his words: "I love you so much." That is why, although I have tried hard, I cannot remember much about that lunch. Anne was wearing a mauve dress, as mauve as the shadows under her eyes, the color of her eyes themselves. My father laughed a lot, and was evidently well pleased with himself. Everything was going well for him. During dessert he announced that he had some shopping to do in the village that afternoon. I smiled to myself. I was tired of the whole thing, and felt fatalistic about it. My one desire was to have a swim.

At four o'clock I went down to the beach. I saw my father on the terrace about to leave for the village; I did not speak to him, not even to warn him to be cautious.

The water was soft and warm. Anne did not appear. I supposed she was busy in her room designing her next collection. Meanwhile my father would be making the most of his time with Elsa. After two hours, when I was tired of sunbathing, I went up to our terrace, and, sitting down in a chair, opened a newspaper.

At that moment Anne appeared from the direction of the woods. She was running, clumsily, heavily, her elbows close to her sides. I had a sudden, ghastly impression of an old woman running toward me, that she was about to fall down. I did not move; she disappeared behind the house, going toward the garage. In a flash I understood and I, too, began running, to catch her.

She was already in her car starting it up. I rushed over and clutched at the door.

"Anne," I cried, "Don't go. It's all a mistake! It's my fault. I'll explain everything!"

She paid no attention to me, but bent to release the brake.

"Anne, we need you!"

She straightened up, and I saw that her face was distorted. She was crying. For the first time I realized that I had hurt a living, sensitive creature, not just a personality. She, too, must once have been a rather secretive small girl, later on an adolescent, and after that a woman. . . . Now she was forty, and all alone. She loved a man, and had hoped to spend ten or twenty happy years with him. As for me . . . that poor miserable face was my doing.

I was petrified. I trembled all over as I leaned against the car door.

"You have no need of anyone," she murmured. "Neither you nor he."

The engine was running. I was desperate; she mustn't go like that!

"Forgive me! I beg you . . ."

"Forgive you! What for?"

The tears were streaming down her face. She did not seem to notice them.

"My poor child!" she said.

She laid her hand against my cheek for a moment. then drove off. I saw her car disappearing around the side of the house. I was irretrievably lost. It had all happened so quickly. I thought again of her face.

I heard steps behind me. It was my father. He had taken the time to remove the imprint of Elsa's lipstick from his face and brush the pine needles from his suit. I turned around and threw myself on him.

"You beast!"

Then I began to sob.

"But what's the matter? Where is Anne? Cécile, tell me! Cécile!"

Chapter 11

MY father and I did not see each other again until dinner time. Both of us were nervous at being suddenly alone together, and neither he nor I had any appetite. We realized we had to get Anne back. I could not bear to think of the look of horror on her face before she left, of her suffering, and my responsibility for it. All my cunning maneuvers and carefully laid plans were forgotten. I was thrown completely off balance, and I could see from his expression that my father felt the same way.

"Do you think," he said, "that she'll stay away from us for long?"

"I expect she's gone back to Paris," I said.

"Paris!" murmured my father in a dreamy voice.

"Perhaps we shall never see her again," I said gloomily.

He seemed at a loss for words, and took my hand across the table.

"You must be terribly angry with me. I don't know what came over me. I was walking back through the woods with Elsa . . . and I . . . ah . . . kissed her, and just at that moment Anne must have come along."

I was not listening. The forms of Elsa and my father embracing under the pines seemed theatrical and unreal to me, and I could not visualize them. The only vivid memory of that day was my last glimpse of Anne's face with its look of grief and betrayal. I took a cigarette from my father's pack and lit it. Smoking during meals was a thing Anne could not bear.

I smiled at my father. "I understand very well. It's not your fault. It was a momentary lapse, as they say. But we must get Anne to forgive us, or rather forgive *you*."

"What shall we do?" he asked me.

He looked far from well. I felt sorry for him and for myself, too. After all, why should Anne act like this, leave us in the lurch, make us suffer so for one little moment of folly?

Hadn't she a duty toward us?

"Let's write to her," I said finally. "Ask her to forgive us."

At last he had found some means of escape from the stupor and remorse of the past three hours. Without waiting to finish our meal, we turned back the tablecloth. My father went to get a lamp, pens and some notepaper. We sat down opposite each other, almost smiling because our preparations had made Anne's return seem probable. A bat was circling around outside the window. My father started writing

An unbearable feeling of disgust and horror rises in me when I think of the letters full of fine sentiments we wrote that evening, sitting under the lamp like two awkward schoolchildren, applying ourselves in silence to the impossible task of getting Anne back. However, we managed to produce two works of art, full of excuses, love and repentance. When I had finished mine, I felt almost certain that Anne would not be able to resist us, and that a reconciliation was imminent. I could already imagine the scene as she forgave us. It would take place in our drawing room in Paris. Anne would come in and. . . .

At that moment the telephone rang. It was ten o'clock. We exchanged a look of astonishment which soon turned to hope. It must be Anne telephoning to say she forgave us and would return. My father bounded to the telephone and called: "Hello!" in a voice full of joy.

Then he said nothing but: "Yes, yes! Where is that? Yes!" in an almost inaudible whisper. I got up, shaken by fear. My father passed his hand over his face automatically. At length he slowly replaced the receiver and turned to me.

"She has had an accident," he said. "On the road to Esterel. It took them some time to discover her address. They telephoned to Paris and got our number from there."

He went on in the same flat voice, and I dared not interrupt.

"The accident happened at the most dangerous spot.

There have been many at that place, it seems. The car rolled down the bluff for about one hundred fifty feet. It would have been a miracle if she had survived."

The rest of the night I remember only as one remembers a nightmare: the road surging up under the headlights, my father's stony face, the entrance to the hospital. My father would not let me see her. I sat on a bench in the waiting room looking at a lithograph of Venice. My mind was a blank. A nurse told me that this was the sixth accident at that spot since the beginning of the summer. It was a long time before my father came back to me.

Then it occurred to me that even in her death, Anne had once more proved how different she was from us. If we had wanted to commit suicide, even supposing we had the courage, it would have been with a bullet in the head, with an explanatory note intended to trouble the sleep of those who had led us to the act. But Anne had made us the magnificent present of allowing us to believe it an accident. A dangerous spot on the road, a car that easily lost balance. It was a gift that we would soon be weak enough to accept. In any case it is a romantic idea of mine to call it suicide. Can one commit suicide on account of people like my father and myself, people who have no need of anybody, living or dead? My father and I never spoke of it to each other as anything but an accident.

The next day we returned to the house at about three o'clock in the afternoon. Elsa and Cyril were waiting for us, sitting on the steps. They seemed like two comic, forgotten characters in the drama. Neither of them had known Anne, or loved her. There they were with their little love affairs, their good looks and their embarrassment. Cyril came up to me and put his hand on my arm. I looked at him: I had never loved him! I had found him sweet and attractive. I had loved the pleasure he gave me, but I did not need him. I was going away, leaving behind me the villa, the garden and that summer. My father was beside me. He took my arm and we went indoors.

In the house were Anne's jacket, her flowers, her room, her scent. My father closed the shutters, took a bottle out of the refrigerator and brought two glasses. It was the only remedy at hand. Our letters of excuse still lay on the table. I pushed them off and they floated to the floor. My father, who was coming toward me holding a full glass, hesitated, then avoided them. I found it symbolical. I took my glass and drained it in one gulp. The room was in half-darkness. I saw my father's shadow on the window. The sea was still beating rhythmically on the shore.

Chapter 12

THE funeral took place in Paris on a fine day. There was the usual crowd of the curious dressed in black. My father and I shook hands with Anne's elderly relations. I looked at them with interest; they would probably have come to tea with us once a year. People cast pitying glances at my father. Webb must have spread the news of his intended marriage. I saw that Cyril was looking for me after the service, but I avoided him. The resentment I felt toward him was quite unjustified, but I could not help it. Everyone was deploring the dreadful, senseless accident, and, as I was still rather doubtful whether it had been an accident, I was relieved.

In the car on the way home, my father took my hand and held it tightly. I thought: "Now we have only each other. We are alone and unhappy." For the first time I cried. My tears were some comfort. They were not at all like the terrible emptiness I had felt in the hospital in front of the picture of Venice. My father gave me his handkerchief without a word. His face was ravaged.

For a month we lived like a widower and an orphan, eating all our meals together and staying at home. Sometimes we spoke of Anne. "Do you remember the day when . . . " We chose our words with care, and averted our eyes for fear we might hurt each other, or that something irreparable would come between us. Our discretion and restraint brought their own recompense. Soon we could speak of Anne in a normal way as of a person dear to us, with whom we could have been happy, but whom God had called to Himself. I have written God, and not fate—but we did not believe in God. In these circumstances we were thankful to believe in fate.

Then one day at a friend's house I met a cousin of hers and liked him and he liked me. For a week I went out with him constantly, and my father, who could not bear to be alone, followed my example with a rather ambitious young woman. Life began to take its old course, as it was bound to. Now, when my father and I are alone together, we joke and discuss our latest conquests. He must suspect that my friendship with Philippe is not platonic, and I know very well that his new friend is costing him too much money. But we are happy. Winter is drawing to an end. We shall not rent the same villa again, but another one, near Juan-les-Pins.

Only when I am in bed, at dawn, listening to the cars passing below in the streets of Paris, my memory betrays me. That summer returns to me with all its memories. Anne, Anne, I repeat over and over again softly in the darkness. Something rises in me that I call to by name, with closed eyes. *Bonjour, tristesse!*

Mais c'est tant pris, si tu es
Triste comment fais tu l'amour,
avec quelqu'un

Après avoir lu
ce livre, je comprends
Vietnamiens
pour ... les préviens ... l'Ecosse.
maintenant bien les ... plus grand

Date Due